# FOUR PAST MIDNIGHT

By

# L. D. K. Johnson

Sale of this book without a front cover may be unauthorized. If this book is coverless, it may have been reported to the publisher as "**unsold** or **destroyed**" and neither the author nor the publisher may have received payment for it.

Copyright © 2013 by L. D. K. Johnson

All rights reserved. No portion of this book may be reproduced in any form without permission from the publisher Belen Books, LLC., except as permitted by U.S. copyright law.

For permission, contact **Belen Books, LLC**.

This is a work of fiction. Names, characters, businesses, places, events, locales, and incidents are either the products of the author's imagination or used in a fictitious manner. Any resemblance to actual people, living or dead, time rifts leading to alternative timelines, or actual events or places is purely coincidental.

**ISBN**: 978-1-959715-24-5

Library of Congress Control Number: **2023947742**
Published by **Belen Books, LLC**
St. Petersburg, FL | Winter Park, FL | Chicago, IL USA
Belenbookspublishing.com

Edited by Beverly R. Waalewyn & Paul Hight
Cover by Belen Media Group

10 9 8 7 6 5 4 3 2

Printed in the United States of America

# For My Husband

And you cannot move at all in Time, you cannot get away from the present moment."

*—The Time Machine*
H. G. Wells

# FOUR PAST MIDNIGHT

# PROLOGUE

Alexandra Martin kept her head low and her dark, brown eyes locked onto Chesterfield High School's non-skid tiles, hoping she could make it to her bus without being harassed by the idiots on the varsity football team. Innocuous enough in her faded jeans, nondescript blue t-shirt, and *Converse* sneakers, she held her breath as she made a beeline past the letterman jacket wearing quartet.

"Well, well, well." Bobby Lieberman's baritone bombarded her senses, the sound of it almost making her trip over her two left feet. "If it isn't *Alexander* Martin."

As usual, the other three laughed at his comment. Annoyed, Alexandra rolled her eyes at what had become a daily occurrence but remained silent. The senior boy was so stupid he couldn't count to twenty-one without using all of his protruding body parts, much less come up with new lame insults on a regular basis.

*Ignore him.*

The thought sounded really good in her mind.

*Just get to your bus and go home.*

*'Easier said than done,'* screamed her Russian DNA, which was in strict conflict with her English ancestry which kept whispering, *'Don't make a scene. Please, don't make a scene.'*

Unfortunately, her Italian-side jumped up dressed as *Don Corleone* from *The Godfather* holding a hatchet and the severed head of a child's wooden rocking horse yelling, *'It's time to go to the mattress!'* and that was the end of getting to the bus without incident.

Stopping midstride, she quickly turned on her heels, facing the troll who had made it his life's ambition to taunt and belittle her. Her blood was boiling. Her temperature was rising. And her inner witch was ready for action.

"Now, Bobby," she sassed, adjusting her glasses more securely on her nose. "It's almost the second nine-weeks of school and all you can say to me is that same old line."

Stunned, Bobby stood in silence, gaping at her precise and unexpected retort.

"Seems to me you need some help on expanding your vocabulary, enhancing your debating techniques, and you need to dislodge your head from your ass."

The other football players gasped, almost sucking all the air out of the narrow hallway.

The sound was music to her ears.

"As you know," she continued. "I can help you with the vocabulary and the debating. However, the head removal you'll have to figure out on your own."

By this time, a sizable group had gathered. Upperclassmen, lower classmen, even a few stoners had stopped to watch the verbal battle, which she was clearly winning. They snickered, pointed, and flung catcalls at the now embarrassed teen. This of course created a warm, fuzzy blanket of confidence that settled over her and she smiled, knowing she had faced the cyclops and was alive to retell the tale.

Bobby, on the other hand, did not share her satisfaction. The tall, freckled-faced boy snarled, nostrils flared, and eyes narrowed to almost non-existent slits of blue fire.

*"You fucking bitch!"* Bobby growled, lunging toward her like he was tackling an opposing player on the field. In response, her brain seized, and eyes shut as she stood waiting for the ground to meet her face.

Needless to say, the last thoughts that flashed through her mind was she was about to die, and she'd never been kissed. Never had a date with a hot guy. Never won an award for doing something amazing, *and* she was going to die a virgin.

*How sad was that?*

After a few agonizing seconds waiting for the two hundred twenty-pound tight end's body to crash into her, she slowly opened her eyes; shocked and relieved to see Roman Giordano, Chesterfield's Junior-Varsity quarterback and team captain, holding the agitated Bobby in a full nelson. His slightly overly long black hair brushing against the collar of his black polo, emerald-green eyes sparkling under the cheap fluorescent lights and looking much too good to be true.

She sighed, releasing the breath she didn't know she was holding.

"Lemme go, Roman!" Bobby kicked, wiggled and cursed, but couldn't get free of the much larger boy's hold. Roman was at least 6'2" compared to Bobby's 5'10" stature, with twenty pounds more lean muscle mass than his opponent. "I'm gonna kick her skinny ass!"

Glancing down and back to confirm her suspicions, she frowned.

"You're not gonna touch her," Roman hissed, voice resembling a feral animal instead of a fifteen-year-old boy.

"Why? Is she your girlfriend or something?" the other boy spat viciously. "You get a hard-on from nerds, Roman?"

That was it. The last thing Bobby Lieberman ever uttered with all of his original teeth. The entire crowd groaned as Roman released him, spun him around, and landed the hardest punch in Chesterfield High School's history. Bobby fell to the floor in a rumpled heap.

"I'll get the nurse!" One astonished teammate yelled as he sprinted down the hallway toward the clinic to get old Nurse Owens.

"Stay right there, Roman!" Principal Jones bellowed as he came jogging around the corner, followed closely by one of the campus security guards and a worried-looking cheerleader who had heard the verbal altercation.

*Freaking great! The sweetest guy in the ninth grade was about to get suspended and it was all her fault.*

# I

*Nine years later...*

"Good morning, Sunshine," Roman sang, as was his normal greeting to her.

His relaxed, well-rested mood only added to her agitated state. Surprisingly, not even his well-tailored, black Armani suit could lighten her foul disposition this rainy autumn day.

"Don't talk to me yet." Alexandra looked down at the growing stack of articles on her cluttered desk.

"Why are you in such a foul mood, Sunshine?"

Her death glare spoke volumes.

Roman chuckled, holding his hands up in surrender as he offered his observation.

"You haven't had your coffee yet." It wasn't a question.

Sullenly, she pouted and shook her head in defeat.

"Here," he stated with that air of confidence she'd always admired. "I picked up an extra-large, double sweet, double shot, mocha latte for you. Enjoy."

She smiled then. A real smile that told him her day had just changed for the better all because of him. Alexandra couldn't help noticing the blush that stole over her best friend's face.

"Okay, enough." Roman waved away her look of appreciation, getting back to the work at hand. "What have you got on the public utility story?"

Mesmerized by his rugged good looks, she watched as he walked around the solid mahogany desk facing an entire wall of glass overlooking Central Park. The view of the bustling city twenty stories below was almost as dazzling as Roman. Mediterranean olive complexion surrounded by eyes the color of the deepest emerald, jet black, silken locks that always fell perfectly into place, and a smile that the Mona Lisa would be jealous of.

The sound of him clearing his throat brought her back to reality.

"Huh?" Alexandra babbled nervously.

"Public works..." Roman's forehead creased.

"You mean the one about the increase in prices for the third year in a row?" she questioned, pretending to look for her notes on the story.

Slowly, he nodded his head.

"I've got a source at the public works department that's dying to spill the beans on his boss's misuse of funds. Guy says the extra money is going towards executive trips to Bora Bora and Botox shots for his wife."

# Four Past Midnight

"Really?" Roman handed her a glazed donut from the brown paper bag he was carrying, not surprised when she practically ripped the golden fried dough ball from his outstretched hand.

"Mmm," she moaned, taking a large bite out of the pastry.

"Good?"

"Mmm hmm," she added with a full mouth, making him laugh.

"Have you spoken to Macintosh about the new stadium that's in the works?"

The construction of the new stadium was the biggest news in town. Not only was the project going to create hundreds of jobs, but it would also bring millions of tourism dollars to the local economy. The city was definitely in need of the additional funds, and all five of the New York city boroughs would benefit from it. It was a win-win situation.

However, the only problem was making sure the facility was built on time, on budget, and constructed safely. No shortcuts. Unfortunately, according to city officials, the money that was supposed to be used for building materials had not been. Their job as journalists was to get the scoop on the missing funds, and that was exactly what he planned to do.

Quickly swallowing, Alexandra informed, "I've got a lunch meeting with him today."

Roman paused, the donut still hovering near his mouth.

"You're having lunch with him?" His voice was gruff.

"Yeah, is that a problem?" she inquired, her brown eyes narrowed at his tone.

He paused again before he answered.

"No, no problem—"

"I'm a professional," Alexandra interrupted.

"I know that you're a professional," his eyes widened.

Leaning forward, she gave him her patented *don't-lie-to-me* stare.

"C'mon, spill it, Roman," she badgered, not backing down.

"It's just the guy's a total sleaze," Roman blurted defensively.

"A sleaze?" she repeated. "And how do you know that?"

"I've heard he's hit on every woman in his department, married, single, and almost retired," he clarified. "Anything in a skirt basically."

"Cool, maybe he'll hit on me," she confessed with a mischievous leer, earning her one of Roman's patented scowls.

"Hey! I'm twenty-three... *single*... never had a boyfriend—"

A confused expression stole across his handsome face as he reminded, "What about Scott Turner the channel six news anchor?"

One perfectly shaped brow hitched at his question.

"Scott Turner only went out with me because he wanted me to do a feature story on him for the *NYC's Up-and-Comers* column," she scoffed indignantly. "He took me out to dinner, talked himself up, and then sent me home in a cab that I had to pay for."

"Why didn't you tell me?" her boss stifled a snicker, not wanting her to be upset.

# Four Past Midnight

"Why? Are you serious?" Alexandra rolled her eyes at him knowing it drove him crazy. "I didn't tell you, *Mr. I'm-God's-Gift*, because not everyone is a magnet for the opposite sex."

"I'm no magnet," Roman blushed. "If you haven't noticed, I've been on a drought lately."

"A year without a girlfriend is not a drought," she informed, feeling even worse about her own love life or lack thereof. "Try a lifetime desert with no rain clouds in sight. Ever."

"Okay, you win," he frowned. "Now, can we get back to work?"

It didn't surprise her that after Roman left, the morning seemed to go a lot smoother. Without the gorgeous editor-in-chief looming over her desk asking questions she had no idea how to answer, everything fell into place.

Lunch with Macintosh gave her all of the information she needed to write a great story on the new sports arena near the Hudson. And to her surprise, the man *accidentally* brushed his palm over her butt.

To her dismay, however, he did not ask her out.

The second meeting was productive as well. Her source at the public works department gave her solid leads on where to track down the missing funds at his company. The only thing that saddened her was that neither man, who were both cute and single, never once gave her a second look.

# L. D. K. Johnson

*Yup, she was definitely not a man-magnet.*

Fortunately, regardless of her inability to attract the opposite sex, her day was still successful and before she knew it, it was almost time to go home.

At five-thirty she began packing her briefcase to leave for her small, but adorable studio apartment in Soho. All she had left was figuring out what to buy for dinner. She wasn't a good cook, even though she came from a long line of incredible Southern cooks. She couldn't even make toast without setting off her smoke detectors.

"Hey!" Roman's deep voice startled her out of her own head. "I just got a call from the owner of the paper, Sylvia Jameson. She wants a mock write up of the public works story with sample photographs and she wants them before midnight.

"No way," she responded, dropping her briefcase back on her desk and plopping onto the seat like a toddler having a tantrum. "I've been here since eight this morning. My body's about to shut down and I think my brain already did. I need a nap."

"Why do you need a nap at five-thirty in the afternoon? Up late partying?" he teased, knowing Alexandra didn't know the meaning of the word party.

"No," she corrected. "I was up late watching reruns of *Forever Knight*."

"Why do I bother asking?"

Her only answer was a dismissive shoulder shrug.

# Four Past Midnight

"Suck it up, Alexandra," he countered, giving a mock pout. "Reporters don't complain about lack of sleep. They're like soldiers. *Comprende?*"

"Did I sign-up to be a news reporter or a marine?" she groaned, unable to hide her disappointment.

"There's no difference," Roman stated with a saucy wink of those emerald orbs accompanied by a huge grin that exposed the dimple on his right cheek. That was all it took to melt her resistance. As usual, it took all of her strength not to swoon.

"Fine, I'll stay," Alexandra agreed, throwing her head back with a dramatic sigh.

"Like you had a choice," Roman teased.

"You better buy me something nice for dinner. I feel my blood sugar plummeting."

"I can't let you fade away," Roman chuckled, his voice deep and smooth. "Thai food, coming up. I'll have it delivered."

Five hours later they were finished. Roman faxed the write-up and within ten minutes the owner was giving him the thumbs-up to print the story. It will be in tomorrow morning's early edition, *Breaking News*. He couldn't help the large grin painted on his face. Ever since he was a little boy, he had loved the idea of running a busy newspaper. It was probably due to all of the *Superman* comic books he read and collected as a child.

"Let's go home, rookie," he announced with a satisfied grin, ushering her out of the office, turning off the lights as they went.

His friend simply nodded.

"Good day's work," he added, patting her on the shoulder. Not realizing his hand lingered a little longer than it should.

Alexandra Martin, aka Sunshine, hadn't changed at all since their freshman year of high school. She still had that sweet smile, great sense of humor, sharp wit, and somehow, she always managed to surprise him. And that was not an easy thing to do.

"So, what are you going to do now?" She slipped into her bright yellow rain jacket that reminded him of a construction worker only not as attractive. The offensive garment covered the lovely plum blouse and form-hugging black pencil skirt she was wearing.

"Nothing much," he mumbled casually, shrugging his shoulders and admiring the top of Alexandra's head. For some reason, he had always been in awe of how shiny and curly it was. Perfect inky spirals except in high humidity weather like tonight. Tonight, it looked like a hot mess. "What about you?"

"Same old same old," she answered in that off-handed way she had. "Do you really have to ask? I'm going to watch reruns of *Forever Knight* and then off to bed."

"Aren't you sick of that show?" he laughed.

"No, it's a classic." The woman glared, reminding him of an errant child. "I love Nick!"

# Four Past Midnight

"You're insane," he smirked, guiding her inside the elevator before following, instinctively checking out her perfectly firm, round ass even though it was now covered.

Alexandra had always had a nice body, but as she matured and gained a few pounds, she was downright delicious.

"It's already late," Roman reminded, not ready to go home yet. "Let's get something at the coffee shop on the corner."

"That sounds good to me," she beamed. "After all, Nick's not going anywhere."

As was their custom, they rode the elevator down to the lobby in comfortable silence, humming along to the muzak playing on the overhead speakers. An instrumental version of *You Give Love a Bad Name* began to play, and they both started doing an air guitar accompaniment in the elevator, not caring if the night watchman saw them on the security camera.

Ten minutes later they were sitting in the practically empty café, chatting and joking at the day's events and past hijinks. Roman laughed until he thought he'd cry when Alexandra told him how she had to bribe one of her contacts in college by flashing her boobs.

"No way!" He wiped away a tear at the corner of his eye. "I can't picture you showing some guy your tits."

"I'm not kidding," she blushed. "I had to get the scoop on the Dean's affair with the women's basketball coach."

"You always surprise me," Roman chuckled.

"Hey, you were right," she said curtly.

"What was I right about?"

"Macintosh," she lowered her voice. "He grabbed my butt, the big pervert."

"He's a guy that saw something nice and wanted to sample the merchandise." Roman dismissively waved away her comment.

*"Eww!"* Alexandra squealed, making a disgusted expression.

This only made him laugh.

"By the way, thanks for the hot chocolate." She took a long sip of the steaming brew. "Nights like this, I miss the year-round warmth of the South."

"I hated those hot summers in Florida," Roman rolled his eyes. "The humidity, the mosquitoes—"

"The theme parks, the friendly people, the beaches," she quickly added, taking another sip. "I thought you loved it there."

He shook his head.

"I tolerated it because my parents decided to move from Manhattan to Clearwater to be near my grandparents. Believe me; I was counting down the years until my eighteenth birthday, so I could go to college wherever I wanted."

That surprised her.

"Really?"

# Four Past Midnight

He nodded.

"I'd dreamt of attending Columbia since I was ten when my elementary school took a field trip to the campus."

Reaching across the table she touched his hand, the contact comforting.

"That's neat you knew from such a young age that you wanted to be a journalist. I didn't know what I wanted to be until my freshman year of college."

"Yeah, seeing all of those hot babes walking around in tight shorts and body-hugging tops," he announced as a glazed look came over his rugged features. "College was definitely for me."

# II

They stayed at the quaint eatery for a few more minutes, hoping the rain would ease, but it refused to. So, they made their way to the corner to wait for the crosswalk signal. You couldn't be too safe crossing the street in the big city. Especially in downtown Manhattan where the cabbies were notoriously fast drivers.

"What time is it?" Roman queried, the rain beating down against the synthetic, black material of his umbrella.

Alexandra pushed the sleeve of her raincoat up a tad to glance at the face of the gold wristwatch she wore.

"Four past midnight," she revealed, readjusting her sleeve once again. "Are you in a hurry to get home to Bruno?"

She giggled.

"Ha, ha!" Roman threw his dark locks back in a mocking laugh, suddenly righted himself and gave her one of his patented *'if-you-weren't-my-best-friend-I'd-kick-your-ass'* glares, which only made her giggle more.

Bruno, his dog, named after Roman's favorite singer Bruno Mars, was a handsome boxer with a wise, old personality, kept his owner on his P's and Q's. The brown and white, two-year old pooch was his pride and joy. And she felt no shame in admitting sometimes she felt a little jealous of the four-legged ball of fur that often-got belly rubs from its owner.

*What she wouldn't do for a belly rub from Roman.*

"At least I have someone to go home to," he taunted.

The well delivered jibe striking her like a punch to the gut.

"Touché," she grimaced, bowing her head in pretend shame. "Maybe I'll get a pet."

"No, absolutely not," Roman scolded, shaking his head. "Remember that goldfish you won at the fair sophomore year and forgot to feed it for over a week?"

A frown marred her lovely face.

"It was so quiet, I forgot I had it until it was too late," she admitted guiltily.

He shook his head again, but this time the motion was accompanied by a frown.

"The poor thing starved to death." She began to defend herself, but he continued, "And don't forget about the pet canary you had in the eleventh grade."

"Was it my fault it flew into the ceiling fan when I accidentally left his cage door open?"

Roman gave her a chastising stare.

"Fine, that was only once."

"What about the hamster senior year?" he asked, emerald eyes narrowing, trying to hide his amusement.

Put on the spot, she nudged him with her elbow, the motion almost made him lose his grip on the umbrella.

"What about the hamster?" she snapped; tone indignant. "I took care of him."

Roman laughed loudly, causing passing pedestrians to glance their way.

"You overfed him and he died of a heart attack after only three months."

Immediately, her hackles rose, and her mouth fell open on a gasp.

"I didn't make him eat all of those food pellets," Alexandra whined. "I think he had an eating disorder, and the pet store covered it up. He showed signs of bulimia."

"What?" he snorted.

"Never mind," she mumbled below her breath realizing she was grasping at straws. "I'm older now, wiser…"

There was only silence as he studied her and she thought he was finished when he suddenly added, "Wait! What about the pet lizard you had in college?"

Her eyes widened in horror.

"That lizard attacked me!" She contorted her hands in an attack position. "To this day I can't look at a lizard without getting the heebie-jeebies."

"A deadly attack lizard?" he scoffed, making her feel like a complete moron.

# Four Past Midnight

"I'm serious," she shuddered. "Those things are dangerous."

Her best friend looked like he was ready to burst out laughing again.

The lizard really did attack her even though she took great care of him. She bought him a roomy glass terrarium and decorated it with a mural of the desert, a couple of plastic cacti and a sturdy piece of driftwood. She even spent her babysitting money on a special heating light to keep his home warm and toasty.

"Fine," she finally conceded. "I guess a pet wouldn't be a good idea. Now that I've reexamined my past track record."

Roman agreed with another nod.

"Thanks for reminding me of my pet failures." A sigh escaped her, and her tone dripped with sarcasm, which she didn't try to hide.

"What are friends for?" he responded robotically, emerald, green eyes sparkling playfully.

"To humiliate you, I'm guessing," she frowned, taking a step forward.

"That was rhetorical," Roman playfully taunted then efficiently adjusted the umbrella over her head.

Finally, the crosswalk signal changed to green and without checking, Alexandra made a motion to step off of the sidewalk into the road. As she stepped down, the loud sound of tires screeching filled the night, as a speeding cab ran through the red light just as she attempted to cross the street. The sound faded quickly as the driver raced away.

"Alexandra are you alright?" Roman questioned, heart pounding in his ears as he wiped away the spray of water the taxi had splashed into his face.

Glancing around the rain-slicked street, he tried to find Alexandra, when a feeling of dread showed its ugly head. As if on cue, the blonde to his left let out a blood curdling scream, the pain-filled sound like nails being run down a chalkboard. Turning in the direction the middle-aged woman was facing, he noticed a bright yellow rain jacket laying over twenty feet away near a construction pylon. Instantly, his chest tightened.

Instinctively, he sprinted toward it. As fast as his legs could go, he ran, ran toward that damn yellow jacket. Horror stole his breath at the sight he found on the garbage-lined Manhattan Street. The scene would forever be etched into his memory.

"Alexandra!" Someone was screaming his friend's name. The woman standing on the corner, it must be her. "Alexandra! Dear father! No!"

It was then he realized the woman was on her cell phone, waving her arms frantically and directing the person on the other end to their location.

"A woman's been hit across from the MetLife building near the Sweetshop Café!" she screeched like a banshee. *"Please hurry!"*

He heard it again, only louder this time.

"Alexandra! *Shit!* Open your eyes!"

Realization dawned; it was him.

# Four Past Midnight

Time stood still as he sat on the cold, wet asphalt cradling Alexandra's limp form in his arms, the fragrance of her perfume wafting around them both. Her dark wet curls clung to the sides of her face, framing it and making her look even more innocent than she already was.

"This can't be happening," Roman sniffled, and his entire body shivered, but he doubted it was from the cold or the falling droplets that was clearing away the remnants of blood that once puddled around his friend's form.

It took forever for the damn paramedics to arrive. Finally, the NYC ambulance pulled up beside him, red lights flashing and siren blaring.

"What took so long?!" he barked at no one in general. "It's been twenty fucking minutes!"

"Sorry, sir," the uniformed woman apologized as she knelt beside him. "There was a construction detour a couple blocks over."

Her expression suddenly softened.

"Sir, please let me help her," the woman coaxed calmly.

Looking down, Roman realized his arms were still wrapped around Alexandra's limp body. The patient EMT had to pry him off her.

"Be gentle with her," he warned, not caring if his tone was harsh.

The woman nodded.

"Of course."

Panic slammed into him at the thought of not being with her. He needed to be with her, didn't want her to open her eyes and not see him. He would have to lie.

"I'm her cousin," he blurted, bloodshot eyes daring her to question him.

"No problem," the emergency medical tech replied, giving him a sympathetic look. "If you want you can ride in the ambulance with her."

Roman released a breath and thanked her as the female EMT and her partner carefully placed Alexandra's body on a stretcher and loaded her into the back of the emergency vehicle. His chest tightened at the sight of her injuries.

*Fuck!*

As expected, the interior of the moving medical unit was packed with monitors, IV's, syringes, antiseptics, and a slew of supplies. It smelled harsh, sterile, and extremely cold. Already queasy, Roman's stomach lurched, and he prayed he wouldn't get sick.

Clearing his throat, he managed to say, "Excuse me, ma'am."

"Call me Maria," she insisted, pointing to her name badge.

"Is she gonna be okay, Maria?" He watched attentively as the highly skilled technician finished attaching Alexandra's IV line.

"I'm not able to say, sir."

## Four Past Midnight

The woman continued her ritual of getting Alexandra's vital signs, securing her with a neck brace, and filling out her medical chart.

"I'm sure the doctor on duty will be able to answer all of your questions." Maria avoided eye contact.

"Okay," he responded uneasily, reaching for his friend's hand, the skin cold and clammy. "You're gonna be fine. I need someone to keep me on the straight and narrow and no one does it better than you, Sunshine."

Gently, Roman brushed her hair out of her eyes, unable to tear his gaze away from the black and blue bruises that formed near her left cheek and temple. On her forehead were multiple gashes both deep and shallow, and the harsh wheezing that accompanied Alexandra's raspy breathing wasn't easing his anxiety at all.

"You'll be fine," he found himself whispering, hoping she'd hear him and open her eyes. "I'll make you a deal. If you hang in there, I'll visit my parents in Florida with you this Christmas."

It was no secret that Alexandra hated the fact he and his dad hadn't spoken for the past five years. It bothered her to the point she would send his father birthday cards and Christmas presents addressed from him. He had scolded her once, insisting it was none of her business, but when the cheeky woman reamed him within an inch of his life, he promptly told her to do what she wanted. He figured she would anyway. Sometimes she was too stubborn for her own good.

As expected, the ambulance ride was tense. Every time the vehicle went over a bump or pothole he worried. It was a relief when they finally arrived at the hospital.

# L. D. K. Johnson

On pins and needles, Roman waited in North General's waiting room for well over an hour. Pacing nervously until he thought he might have worn a path in the cheap linoleum. All the while, silently mumbling a prayer, something he hadn't done since he was a teenager. It was difficult to remember he was once an altar boy. Surely, Sister Camilla would have made him do penance if she knew.

"Mr. Giordano?" A male voice came from near the doorway. The man's green surgical scrubs informed of his doctor's status.

His entire body tensed as he braced himself for the news.

"Yes, that's me." He felt his stomach lurch again at the doctor's uneasy manner.

"I'm Doctor Reed—"

"How is she?" he stopped the man in midsentence, tired of aimless chit-chat. "May I see her now? I'm the only family she's got in town. I don't want her alone when she wakes."

"I'm afraid I have some bad news," the elder blonde man informed clearing his throat.

Roman felt the pit in his stomach deepen and his temple begin to throb a wild beat.

"She... she d-didn't make it." It wasn't a question.

Uncomfortably, the doctor looked down at his chart and shook his head. That did it. Unexpectedly, the room moved under his feet, and he stumbled onto his knees. The entire space spun like a washing machine stuck on the spin cycle, and he could have sworn he heard a crack of lightning and a boom of thunder come from outside then realized he had knocked down a metal hospital cart and the lamp on a nearby end table.

From somewhere close, he heard the doctor shouting for a wheelchair and a nurse. It was the last sound he heard before the world turned black.

*'I need a psychiatric resident to the fifth floor, STAT!'* The garbled voice on the hospital's paging system woke him from a restless slumber.

Slowly, he looked around and wasn't surprised he was on a gurney near the nurse's station across from the waiting room. Adjacent to where he lay, a small carton of orange juice and a chocolate-chip cookie waited for him. Completely parched, he chugged down all of the juice hoping it would give him the strength to stand. After a few minutes, he was finally able to even though his legs felt like wet spaghetti noodles. He left the cookie on the tray since his stomach was too upset to eat it without suffering the consequences.

For a moment, he stood contemplating his next move. He didn't want to leave the safety of the hospital. Not yet. He didn't have the strength or desire to go home and call Mr. and Mrs. Martin to tell them their only daughter... *only child*... was never coming back home. Never going to grace them with one of her dazzling smiles, or in his case a disapproving scowl.

"It's my fault, damn it!" he mumbled under his breath. "She'd still be alive if I hadn't offered her the stupid position at the newspaper. She would be safe now teaching at Chesterfield High

School's English department. She'd be alive and I'd still have my best friend."

Unable to control his despair any longer, he allowed hot waves of tears to flow down his face, not caring who saw. Brushing them away angrily, he began to wander aimlessly around the quiet hospital hallways. Halfway down the hallway a third-shift nurse, who had assisted Dr. Reed when he fell, saw him. Her kind smile made him want to curl up into a ball on the floor and disappear.

"Sir," she stated in a hushed tone, handing him a cup of hot coffee from a nearby dispenser. "You shouldn't be wandering around this area, it's restricted."

Looking up, he noticed a sign on the door stating *Employees Only*.

"I'm sorry."

"Do you want me to call you a cab?" She frowned, which revealed the worry-lines marring her forehead.

Unable to form a coherent thought, he shook his head.

"You can't stay here all night," the woman added.

"I know, but I can't go home," Roman said with a shaky voice. "Not yet."

"The young woman who passed away, was she your girlfriend?" The nurse laid a comforting hand to his shoulder.

"No," he uttered as his heart clenched in his chest. "She was my best friend."

"I see." Her expression softened. "I'm so sorry for your loss."

# Four Past Midnight

"Thanks," he whispered, glancing away.

Truthfully, he had always abhorred that phrase. Why did everyone say that when someone lost a loved one? *'I'm sorry for your loss'.* Were they really, or were they glad it was your loss and not theirs?

"Listen, why don't you go up to the chapel?" the woman encouraged. "It's on the third floor. It's nice and quiet there. Maybe saying a prayer might help you feel better. Sometimes when I've had a tough time, I like to stop in and light a candle and put the events of the day into perspective. For some reason, it always makes me feel better."

He nodded in agreement, and then obediently followed the nurse to the small hospital chapel.

"Thank you." The kind nurse turned to leave, but before she could reach the end of the corridor he called out, "I'm sorry I didn't catch your name."

"It's Olivia Marshall," she informed with a warm smile.

"Thank you, Nurse Marshall." Roman gave a small smile back.

"You are more than welcome," Olivia replied then resumed her path down the hall, leaving him alone with his misery.

Hesitantly, he entered the small room and slowly took in his surroundings. The softly muted color scheme of the Spanish-styled chapel, the soft glow of the candles, the oversized chunky wooden cross only added to his apprehension, but he still went inside. After he had left for college, he stopped attending religious services of any kind. He didn't exactly know why. Perhaps he had just grown out of it. Regardless, he felt out of his element.

Glancing around, he sighed. It was only him in the quiet space and that made him feel worse. Exhausted and weak from grief, dread battered his mind as he chose a pew near the front by the burning candles. Heat radiated from them, reminding him his suit was still damp from the rain. Visions of Alexandra's limp form flashed through his brain causing the tears to flow once more and he let them. He let them run down his face until his eyes burned from it, until his chest constricted, and he felt numb.

Overwhelmed with despair, he sobbed to the point he could barely catch his breath, the pained sound echoing within the confines of the intimate space.

Finally, he knelt.

"How do I start?" he whispered to the crucifix adorning the front of the chapel.

Thank goodness it didn't answer back.

"Dear father, please forgive me," Roman started, his hands clenched together in supplication. "I haven't done this in a very long time, but I need to do this now…"

# III

*Beep! Beep! Beep!*

"What the hell?!" Roman jerked awake, a thin layer of sweat covering his body, covers twisted like gnarled branches around his legs.

The alarm blared as irritation immediately spread through his already racing mind.

*Damn it!*

He remembered his early meeting at the newspaper with, "Alexandra."

Sitting up, he acknowledged his sheets looked like he had been twisting and turning like a tornado. Red-rimmed eyes burned as if he hadn't slept at all.

*What day was it?*

Glancing at the clock, he saw it was Tuesday, October 22… *Again?*

"It was just a nightmare, wasn't it?" he mumbled to Bruno who was asleep at the foot of his king-sized bed. The dog looked up and gave him a reassuring bark.

He stilled. An overwhelming feeling this had already happened descended upon him, almost stifling the shaky breath he tried to inhale. Lungs having difficulty filling like someone had punctured them with an ice pick.

*It was only a nightmare.*

Or was it?

Still in a sleep-drunk haze, he threw his legs over the side of the bed, pushing himself to a standing position, when his size twelve feet hit the plush carpet below. Slowly, he walked to the ensuite bathroom and *wasn't* surprised to complete his morning ritual of showering, shaving, brushing his teeth, and styling his hair in only twenty minutes.

Standing inside of his walk-in closet, he already knew which suit, shirt, and tie to wear, his favorite black Armani suit, pale blue button-down dress shirt, and a blue, black, and gray tie with geometric shapes on it. Once more his thoughts drifted to the nightmare that plagued his sleep, grimacing as he remembered the part of the dream when Alexandria lay bleeding in his arms, the pungent smell of the city along with her softly scented *Chanel* perfume suddenly attacked his mind. Brushing it away like he would an annoying gnat, he continued getting dressed.

The morning hadn't started well for Alexandra.

It sucked, actually.

# Four Past Midnight

First, the alarm clock she bought for a steal of three dollars never sounded, which in turn had her running fifteen minutes behind schedule. She had never been late for work in her entire life. Never. And it bothered her to think she might not make it into the office before Roman. She was OCD in that respect.

Second, the hot water system of her one-hundred-year-old apartment building was on the fritz, *again*. It was pure torture having to take a shower in frigid water. She swore icicles were forming on the tip of her nose. The building superintendent was going to get an earful the next time she saw him.

Next, her brand-new coffeemaker that she had bought at a department store's going out of business sale, dripped out only five drops of brownish-gray liquid, then sputtered and clanked and refused to work. Thirty dollars down the proverbial drain.

*Great!*

Still, with all of those obstacles she searched her closet for something nice to wear for her early meeting with Roman at the office. Roman always looked so fashionable is his expensive, imported Italian suits that hugged his well-chiseled body in all the right places. His dress shirts always perfectly pressed and matched to his tie. The three-hundred-dollar shoes didn't hurt either.

"I really need to get some more clothes," she grumbled, hands perched high on her hips as she stared at an unimpressive wardrobe. Half of her clothes were too tight, the other half out of date. The former problem she was certain to be caused by eating too many chocolate-chip muffins from the café.

Roman had invited her to join the gym located on the ground floor of his upscale apartment complex, but she was too embarrassed to workout with him. The man had a body made for sin. Every inch of the *Italian Stallion* was hard, unyielding, and drop-dead gorgeous. There was no way she'd ever let him see her muffin-top and flabby arms.

After a few minutes of staring into the sparse space, she gave up. It was back to her conservative, black pencil skirt and plumb button-down silk blouse that enhanced her complexion and made her chocolate-brown eyes look more exotic. The entire ensemble paired with simple black flats, since she was much too clumsy to wear high heels.

Adding to her frustration, even her hair was being difficult today, the humidity causing it to expand and frizz until she resembled a French poodle. In desperation, she searched under her sink until she found her anti-frizz solution and styling gel, the bottles hadn't been opened yet. No wonder she was always a hot mess. With a steady hand, she applied the styling products to no avail. Then in a huff, she grabbed a rubber band and put the entire curly mess into a high ponytail.

*Great! Just great!*

Finally, she applied eyeliner and mascara which brought out the rich brown of her irises and a thin layer of nude lip gloss that made her naturally full lips seem even fuller. At least her complexion was acceptable. She'd never needed to wear concealer or foundation since she'd been blessed with clear, perfect skin. In her opinion, it was her one saving grace.

She smiled at her reflection. It wasn't *Covergirl* perfection, but it wasn't *Jabba the Hutt* either.

## Four Past Midnight

Glancing at the clock one more time, she grinned. Ready in only fifteen minutes. She was sure to beat Mr. GQ to the office.

*Ha! Her record would still be intact!*

---

"Good morning, Alexandra," Roman acknowledged weakly, which was *not* his normal greeting to her.

Suspicious eyes narrowed at the man she'd known for almost a decade.

"How did you just greet me?"

"What are you talking about?" Roman bristled.

"You said, 'Good morning, Alexandra,'" she mimicked in her best baritone.

"So," his scowl deepened.

"Ever since the ninth grade you've always said, 'Good morning, Sunshine.' Always."

Large, muscular shoulders shrugged in a dismissive gesture.

"Oh, well."

His perturbed mood only added to her already agitated state. Surprisingly, not even his well-tailored, black Armani suit could lighten her foul disposition this rainy autumn day.

Sitting forward in her chair, she glared at him.

"What's wrong with you this morning?"

"Nothing," he claimed, scrubbing one hand over his face. A motion she recognized he only did when upset. If he rubbed the nape of his neck next, she'd know he was in no joking mood.

"If you want to talk about it, you can," she encouraged, hating to see him upset.

"I said nothing is wrong, Alexandra!" he barked, rubbing the nape of his neck. "Are you deaf?"

She gaped in shock. He'd never spoken to her like that before. In all the years they had been friends he had always spoken to her with respect.

"Fine, be like that! Don't talk to me anymore before I slap the moodiness off of your face." Alexandra looked back down at the growing stack of articles on her cluttered desk. The need to do something violent to him suddenly became a viable option.

A loud, frustrated sigh escaped his lips when realization dawn about what he had just done. Immediately, he was embarrassed and ashamed. Alexandra was one of the people he cared the most for, and she didn't need to be yelled at or disrespected.

"I'm sorry... Sunshine," he apologized in a softer tone, wishing he could take it back.

The death glare she shot him spoke volumes, and he wasn't surprised. He deserved it.

Roman chuckled and held his hands up in surrender.

"I haven't been sleeping well the last few nights," he tried to explain, yet Alexandra still glared at him.

# Four Past Midnight

"I see you haven't had your coffee yet." It wasn't a question.

At last, she pouted and shook her head in defeat.

"Here you go," he stated with that air of confidence she'd always admired. "I picked up an extra-large, double sweet, double shot, mocha latte for you. Enjoy!"

Suddenly Roman stopped. As he looked around, his head filled with images of the exact scene. *This had happened before.*

"What's wrong?" she asked, frowning.

"Huh?"

"*You*... are you alright?" she queried; her expression grim. "It's like you zoned-out for a moment and you haven't been acting like your usual chipper self."

Shaking his head, he massaged his nape again, the tense muscles bothering him.

"Have you ever had that feeling you've done something before?"

"Explain," the intelligent female immediately shifted into reporter mode.

"You know, when you do or say something and it feels like you've already done it," he rambled. "I'm sure we've had this conversation before. I'm positive of it."

After a few seconds she answered.

"Yeah," she replied. "I know what you're talking about. It's called *déjà vu*."

"That's it," he exhaled with a scowl. "Right now, our conversation feels like déjà vu."

"Maybe, all of this," she waved her arms around in undulating waves, "is a lab on an alien space station where they are studying our human bodies so they can clone us."

With that said, she stuck two pencils in her hair and stuck a neon post-it on her forehead and pretended to be a space alien from the planet Zarf, making him laugh out loud.

"I have no idea why I keep you around," Roman teased, finally relaxing.

"I think it's because no one else will put up with your crap," she smirked, removing her *'antennae'* and the paper.

"It's a strong possibility," he chuckled, feeling more of his anxiety melt away.

She smiled then; a real smile that told him her day had just changed for the better all because of him. Alexandra couldn't help but notice the blush that stole over her best friend's face.

"Stop looking at me like that and drink your coffee before the damn thing gets cold," he ordered, suddenly feeling uncomfortable.

Appreciatively, she took the disposable plastic travel cup from his hands.

"Thank you, boss," she purred with a devilish wink.

The action made him blush again.

"You look very handsome today, but then again you always do."

His eyes narrowed suspiciously at her comment.

"I mean… you always take the time to look your best, unlike me," Alexandra quickly backtracked.

"I think you look very nice this morning too," he complimented, taking in her appearance. "Although, you've worn this particular outfit quite a bit lately."

"I haven't worn this outfit in over a month," she claimed with a look of confusion.

"Oh," he mumbled, suddenly uncomfortable. Changing the mood of the conversation he added, "Well, you look great regardless."

His flattering remark surprised her.

"I do?"

"Yeah, that shade of purple brings out your naturally tanned complexion and also makes your eyes almost hypnotic," Roman sincerely expressed.

"Wow!" she teased. "I should yell at you more often."

"Okay, enough," he smirked, waving away her look of appreciation, getting back to the work at hand. "What have you got on the public utility story?"

Immediately, his eyes glanced over the large stack of papers on her cluttered desk. He never understood how she could work in such disarray when she was OCD about everything else in life being perfect.

Alexandra, on the other hand, mesmerized by his graceful movements, watched as he walked around the solid mahogany desk facing an entire wall of glass overlooking Central Park. Thin strands of sunlight filtered through the mini blinds illuminating Roman's expressive, emerald eyes. The view of the bustling city twenty stories below was nowhere near as dazzling as he was. Against her will, her mouth went dry, and her nether regions dampened.

"Alexandra Maria Martin are you awake yet?" he asked then cleared his throat to get her attention.

"Huh?" She subtly checked her chin for drool.

Taken aback by her lack of focus, his forehead creased.

"Who's zoning out now?" he grinned. "The public works story, how's it going?"

Completely embarrassed, she pretended to look for her notes on the story.

"You mean the one about the increase in prices for the third year in a row?"

Her editor nodded in response.

"I've got a source at the public works department that's dying to spill the beans on his boss's misuse of funds," Alexandra smiled. "Guy says the extra money is going towards executive trips to Bora Bora and Botox shots for his wife. Can you believe it?"

Roman shook his head.

"Who in the world would want Botox shots?" Stopping for a moment, she continued, hardly taking in a breath. "It's a deadly toxin you know, made from botulin. Who thinks up these things? Men, that's who."

Alexandra's tirade made him grin.

Her rant ceased when she noticed him staring at her strangely.

"Just a bit of useless trivia," she grumbled with a wave of her hand.

"FYI: I already knew that," he confessed, looking away.

Before she could start a new topic, Roman offered her a glazed donut from the brown paper bag he was carrying. He wasn't surprised when the woman practically ripped the deep-fried sugary confection from his extended hand.

"Mmm," she moaned, taking a large bite out of the pastry, chewed, and then swallowed. "I really and truly love that you feed me."

"Is it good?" Roman suppressed a laugh.

Ravenously, she took another bite.

"Mmm-hmm," she confirmed with a full mouth, making him release the laugh he had been trying to keep inside. He hadn't even known that he was staring at her. At her mouth actually… which made her self-conscious.

Quickly, she swallowed.

"Why are you staring?" She brushed her fingertips over her lips in case donut crumbs had gathered there. "Is there something on my mouth?"

He heard her, but for some reason, he couldn't tear his gaze away from her soft, pouty lips.

*What the hell was he doing? Ogling his best friend's lips? He was going straight to hell!*

"You have a piece of…"

"What do I have—"

Without thought, he leaned over her desk, and removed the small crumb with his slightly calloused thumb.

"There, all gone," he notified, thumb still lingering on her lips. "You really do look nice today. Beautiful actually."

"Thank you." Her voice cracked as she pulled away, looking down at her messy desk to hide the blush threatening to reveal her true feelings for him.

Once more, he cleared his throat.

"Have you spoken to Macintosh about the new stadium in the works?" his employee swallowed and was about to answer when he answered for her. "Wait, don't tell me. You've got a meeting with him today."

Roman paused, the donut still hovering near his mouth.

"You're also having lunch with him," voice gruff and menacing.

The idea of her spending time with another guy, even if it was work related, made him suspicious. He'd never felt territorial over Alexandra before, so why would he be suspicious of another guy's intentions toward his best friend now?

# Four Past Midnight

*Weird.*

"Yeah," her eyes narrowed, and lovely lips pursed. "Do you think that's going to be a problem? If you're worried, I can—"

"No, no problem at all." He paused again, eyes going to the vee of her plumb-colored blouse instead. "And you don't even have to ask, I know that you are a professional."

*Dear heaven! What was wrong with him this morning?*

Now agitated, Alexandra began to tap her foot and folded her arms across her chest in a defensive posture.

"How did you know what I was going to say? Have you been going through my calendar again?"

Nodding his head he reminded, "I've told you; this has all happened before. I can't explain it, but it's true."

"Weird," she whispered. "So why shouldn't I have lunch with this guy? Spill it, Roman."

Evasively, he folded his arms across his chest.

"The guy's a total sleazeball, that's all," he said, trying to get his eyes to focus on her face instead of her breasts.

"Why is he a sleazeball?" she interrogated, taking a long swallow of her latte.

"I've heard he's hit on every woman in his department, married, single, and almost retired… anything in a skirt basically," Roman blurted, feeling protective. "I've also heard he has used his female contacts to procure favors. *And* at lunch he's gonna grab your ass."

Alexandra almost spat her beverage all over her desk, but managed to regain her composure as she coughed to clear her throat.

When she was finally able to respond, she sputtered, "I guess he's just like you."

"Wait a minute," Roman protested, offended by her comment. "I've never grabbed your ass."

"That's not what I meant," she clarified as she reached for a paper napkin stashed in her top desk drawer.

"I may be a lot of things, but I don't grab women's asses… unless I've been given permission," he corrected. "And I don't use women."

He grinned.

"Women use *me*… for my *mind*… for my *body*," he boasted playfully as he flexed his bicep. The simple pose making her want to rip off his clothes and ravage him on top of her desk.

"Cool, maybe he'll hit on me and ask me out," Alexandra giggled and added a mischievous leer for emphasis.

Roman could only give her one of his patented scowls.

"I'm twenty-three-years-old… I'm still single… I've never had a boyfriend—"

"What about Scott Turner the channel six news anchor?" he questioned, leaning against her desk as if he owned it. "I thought you two were dating."

*He knew they weren't.*

One of her perfectly shaped brows arched.

# Four Past Midnight

"Scott Turner is a weenie," she hissed. "He only went out with me because he wanted me to do a feature story on him for the *NYC's Up-and-Comers* column. He took me to dinner at The Dutch—"

A low whistle passed his beautifully formed lips.

"The restaurant near your place that's so popular you have to make reservations months in advance?" Roman interrogated.

Suspicion ate away at the other man's intentions toward his Alexandra. *No.* Not his Alexandra.

"That's the one," she snorted, the sound making him laugh.

"Then what happened?" Curiosity got the best of him.

She took another sip of her beverage then added, "In a nutshell, he talked himself up, and then sent me home in a cab."

"No way!" Roman shook his head in disbelief.

"It's true *and* I had to pay the cab fare myself!" his partner in crime gawked.

*"What a prick!"* he practically growled. Secretly glad the man didn't try to make a move on her.

Alexandra nodded in agreement.

"Plus, he's not my type anyway," she confirmed with a graceful wave.

"I'm shocked you didn't tell me this before. Why didn't you say something?" Roman inquired. "Wait a minute. What's your type?"

"Why? Are you serious?" She rolled her eyes at him knowing it drove him crazy, choosing to avoid his question about her type of man.

What was she supposed to say? *You're my kind of man.* Yeah. Right.

"I didn't tell you, *'Mr. I'm-God's-Gift'*, because not everyone is a magnet for the opposite sex."

With an icy glare he protested, "I'm no magnet. If you haven't noticed, I've been on a drought lately."

"Don't make me laugh. A year without a girlfriend is not a drought," she informed, feeling even worse about her own love life or lack thereof. "Try a lifetime desert with no rain clouds in sight. Ever."

Hearing those words, Roman gave her a chastising stare, but kept his comments to himself since she was already riled up.

"Think about that before you complain about a lack of a love life," Alexandra snapped. "You're single by choice. I'm single because the universe hates me."

"The universe doesn't hate you," he honestly educated. "You're too picky."

"I'm not too picky," she gasped, eyes sparkling defiantly. "I believe in love and long-term commitment. Not one-night stands with someone who won't remember my name in the morning. And I definitely don't want to do the walk-of-shame out of some random guy's apartment."

At this, his emerald gaze narrowed.

"So, you're going to stay single forever?"

Roman couldn't imagine Alexandra staying single. She was much too nurturing and compassionate not to share her life with someone special. Even with him, she often kept him on task, made sure he ate regularly, and she always took the time to ask him how his day was going. It wasn't the big things she did, it was all the many little things.

"Probably," Alexandra huffed, secretly wishing that wouldn't be the case.

"Yeah, you're right. That is pretty pathetic," he concurred without heat. "Now can we get back to work?"

After Roman left her office the morning seemed to go a lot smoother. Without the gorgeous editor-in-chief looming over her desk asking questions she had no idea how to answer and staring at her peculiarly, everything fell into place.

For the life of her, she couldn't figure out why he was acting so strangely.

Lunch at *E.A.T.* on Madison Avenue with Macintosh gave her all of the information she needed to write a terrific article on the new sports arena near the Hudson. And to her surprise, the man did *accidentally* brush his palm over her butt.

To her dismay, however, he didn't ask her out.

The food was terrific though, as always. She had the savory Quiche Lorraine, a fresh green salad, and a soda. The freshly baked bread though stole the show.

Her second meeting also went off without a hitch. Her source at the public works department kept his hands to himself and also gave her solid leads on where to track down the missing funds at his company. The only thing that saddened her was that neither man, who were both cute and single, never once gave her a second look. Yup! She was definitely *not* a man magnet.

On a happier note, regardless of her inability to attract the opposite sex, her day was still productive, and before she knew it, it was time to call it quits. At thirty minutes past five o'clock, Alexandra began packing her briefcase to go home to her small, yet adorably furnished studio apartment in Soho. All the while debating between Chinese food or pizza for dinner. She wasn't a good cook, even though she came from an extensive line of amazing Southern chefs. Truth be told, she couldn't even make toast without setting off the smoke detectors in her apartment.

"I have some bad news, Sunshine," Roman's deep voice startled her out of her own head. "Sylvia just called. She wants a mock write up of the public works story with sample photos and she wants them before midnight. We're gonna have to put in some overtime hours. Sorry."

"That's ridiculous," she responded, dropping her black patent leather briefcase back on her desk and plopping onto the seat like a teenager pulling an attitude. "I've been here since eight this morning. I'm exhausted. Did you know *this* was going to happen *too*?"

He ignored the last part of her question.

## Four Past Midnight

"Next time, you'll know not to stay up late during the week to watch a damn *Forever Knight* marathon," he scolded, ending his statement with a wink to soften the blow.

"Sure, Dad," she provoked, sticking out her tongue at him.

Unbeknown to Alexandra, it took all of his self-control not to grab her and kiss the living daylights out of her. Instead, he shook his head.

Then against his wishes, his member hardened at the idea of kissing her.

"This entire day seems so strangely familiar," he huffed his frustration. "It's really starting to irritate me now."

Alexandra suddenly stopped spinning around in her office chair.

"How did you know I was up late watching *Forever Knight* reruns?"

The only thing he could do was shrug his shoulders.

"Don't worry. The day's almost over," she consoled. "Do we really have to work overtime? Can't we submit the article tomorrow morning instead? I need to get some rest."

Roman gave her a mock pout.

"Don't whine, Alexandra. Real reporters like Diane Sawyer and Christiane Amanpour don't complain about lack of sleep. They're like soldiers, comprende?"

"I signed-up to be a news reporter not a marine," his coworker sassed with a growing frown.

"There's no difference." He chuckled and winked then gave a huge grin exposing the dimple on his right cheek. It took all of her strength not to let him see her swoon.

"Fine, I'll stay," she agreed with a pout.

"Like you really had a choice." He smirked.

"You better buy me something nice for dinner."

"I can order a pizza from Joe's," Roman smiled, happy to have memorized the popular restaurant's phone number.

To his surprise, Alexandra shook her head.

"What about Thai food?" she suggested out of the blue, suddenly craving a plate of *Pad Kra Pao Moo*. A savory dish that consisted of stir-fried ground pork with a ton of spicy chilies, pungent garlic, onions, green beans, and Thai basil served over rice. Of course, she would follow it up with her favorite Thai desserts: *Khao Niew Mamuang* which was a simple, traditional Thai dessert made by pairing ripe mangos with sweetened sticky rice served with coconut milk.

She wasn't surprised when her stomach growled.

Roman instantly froze with that same odd feeling he had been experiencing all day.

"No, I'm not in the mood for Thai tonight," he blurted rather abruptly.

Her eyes widened at his proclamation.

"That's shocking," Alexandra countered.

"Why?"

# Four Past Midnight

"You've never turned down Thai food," the journalist's demeanor hardened. "You eat Pad Thai at least twice a week."

"Yeah, that's why I'm sick of it," he lied, unable to tell her he'd eaten it several nights in a row in his dream.

"Pizza it is then," Alexandra conceded unable to debate his logic. "Could you order a large sausage and pepperoni with extra cheese?"

"Anything for you." Roman grinned.

# IV

Approximately five hours later they were finished. Roman faxed the write-up and within ten minutes the owner was giving him the thumbs-up to print the story, but instead of feeling proud he felt a sinking feeling in the pit of his stomach.

"Why do you look like you're about to lose your dinner?" Alexandra asked when she noticed his discomfort.

"The pizza didn't agree with me," he fibbed, averting his gaze.

"So…" Alexandra stood stretching her arms above her head trying to relieve some of the tension in her arms, back, and shoulders. "Did Sylvia like the article?"

A broad grin appeared on his face.

"It'll be in tomorrow morning's early edition… *Breaking News*." The thought of Alexandra not seeing their article made him grimace and he couldn't help the worried expression that settled on his face.

"Hey!" She tapped his shoulder. "Don't look so concerned. The readers are gonna love it. I promise."

"I'm sure they will." He tried to smile but couldn't. "Let's go home, rookie."

## Four Past Midnight

Roman ushered her out of the office, turning off the lights as they went.

"Great work today, by the way," he added, maneuvering her with a firm hand placed at the small of her back right above her ass, purposely letting his hand linger a little longer than it should.

"Are you trying to cop a feel, Mr. Giordano?" she asked with a chuckle.

Alexandra Martin, aka Sunshine, hadn't changed at all since their freshman year of high school. She still had that cute smile (without her braces), a great sense of humor, and sharp wit. And she never hesitated to put him in his place. He loved that about her.

"Maybe," he answered truthfully. The idea of touching her was definitely appealing. "Would you mind if I did?"

She giggled at the thought. The heartthrob she'd lusted after since the ninth grade wanting to grab her ass.

*Ha!*

"Very funny," Alexandra blushed at the preposterous notion. "I'm not your type."

"There you go with that *'type'* thing again," Roman's voice lowered.

"In all of the years I've known you, you've only dated tall, long-legged, voluptuous goddesses," she scoffed rather indignantly.

"Really?" he grinned. "I hadn't noticed."

Truth be told, he was flattered she had taken the time to learn his dating patterns.

"So, what are you going to do now?" the work-worn woman slipped into her bright yellow rain jacket that reminded him of a construction worker only not as attractive. Unfortunately, the incorrigible garment blocked his view of her ample chest and delectable ass.

"Nothing much, maybe I'll watch a movie or a game on cable. I have a few college games I recorded on my DVR I can watch." he shrugged his shoulders while admiring the top of Alexandra's head.

Roman didn't know why, but he'd always been in awe of how shiny and curly it was. Perfect inky spirals except in high humidity weather like tonight. Tonight, it would have looked like a hot mess if it hadn't been secured into a ponytail.

"What about you?" he questioned.

"Same old same old," she answered in that off-handed way she had. "Do you really have to ask?"

"I forgot," he said, laughing. "You're going home to watch reruns of *Forever Knight*' and then off to bed. Am I correct?"

"You know me too well," she smirked.

"Aren't you sick of that show?" he asked as he adjusted his trench coat.

Alexandra had gotten hooked on the show during their junior year of high school. He'd made the mistake of buying her all three seasons on DVD last Christmas. Now, all she wanted to do was rush home to look at them. His friend needed to get a boyfriend. Wait. Not a boyfriend. A hobby…

Her face lit up at the idea of watching the episodes as soon as she got home.

"Of course not, it's a cult classic," Alexandra explained. "I've been watching those shows since I was a teenager."

"Yes. I know," his words accompanied by an eye roll.

"Anyway, I love Nick," she unapologetically gushed. "He's yummy."

"There are other vampire shows out there, you know," Roman smirked, guiding her inside the elevator before following, instinctively checking out her perfectly firm, round ass even though it was now covered.

Alexandra always had an appealing body, but as she matured and gained a few pounds, she was downright delicious. For some reason, her ass looked extra tempting and tonight he wanted to grab it. In reality, he would never try too, but a man could dream.

"It's already late, do you wanna go somewhere to hangout?" he begged, trying to conceal his guilty thoughts, not ready to go home yet.

"Let's get something at the coffee shop on the corner," she beamed. "I have a craving for their mint hot chocolate with real whipped cream and dark chocolate shavings."

His chest tightened, wanting to change the flow of their evening.

"Why don't we try somewhere else?" Desperation fueled his words. "What about Monty's?"

"Monty's?" Her eyes narrowed. "Isn't that a pick-up joint?"

The last time they visited that establishment, Roman was immediately approached by several extremely attractive women ranging in age from early twenties to late sixties. All of them ignored her while they chatted and flirted with her best friend and when he began programming all their cell numbers into his phone, she snuck out, and caught a *Lyft* home.

Adamantly, she shook her head no.

"C'mon," Alexandra begged. "I'm dying for their hot chocolate."

Her choice of the word *dying* didn't sit well with him, but reluctantly, he gave in.

"I guess some hot chocolate would be nice on a rainy night like this," he grinned, wanting her to be happy. "But next time I get to choose our venue."

"Whatever you say, boss." She grinned.

"However, this time it's your treat," he beamed smugly.

The curious look she shot him made him uneasy.

"This time?" Alexandra appeared puzzled.

"Never mind." Clearing his throat, he thought of something to say to change the subject, but nothing came to mind except, "So, you're paying tonight?"

Alexandra nodded, dark curls bouncing.

"Sure, it'll be my treat," she grinned. "After all, Nick's not going anywhere."

# Four Past Midnight

Like before, they rode the elevator down to the lobby in relaxed silence. Alexandra hummed along to the muzak playing on the overhead speakers while Roman stood uneasily pleading with the universe to give him a break. As the lift continued its smooth descent, an instrumental version of *You Give Love a Bad Name* started, but only she started doing an air guitar accompaniment, not caring if the night watchman saw her on the security camera.

"What's the matter?" Alexandra pouted. "We always play air guitar to Bon Jovi."

"I'm sick of this song that's all," he lied unsuccessfully. "The radio stations overplay it."

Alexandra frowned at his ridiculous response.

*Pff!*

Bon Jovi could never be overplayed!

Roughly ten minutes later they were sitting in the practically empty café, chatting and joking, at the day's events and past high jinks. Roman laughed until he thought he would cry when Alexandra told him how she had to bribe one of her college contacts by flashing her boobs.

"I still can't believe you did that!" He wiped away a tear at the corner of his right eye. "Why would you show some horny college student your tits? You're kidding."

"I'm not kidding," Alexandra blushed. "I was determined to get the scoop on the Dean's affair with the women's basketball coach, Mrs. Reynolds, and his perverted assistant kept eyeing my chest."

He smiled, a smile that made her want to jump across the table and have her way with him right there in the café. Unfortunately, she stayed in her seat and settled for admiring his hotness from a distance.

"It was my duty as a reporter," she continued with renewed zeal. "I would have lost the story if I hadn't."

"I would have loved to see that," her best friend chuckled until his sides ached.

"See what? My boobs?" She blushed at the thought of Roman seeing her naked.

"I'm a guy, of course I wanna see your boobs," he expounded then tried to backtrack. "I only meant you always surprise me."

"Is that a good or bad thing?" she pressed wanting to know what he thought of her, her face sporting a frown.

"It's good," he reassured with a playful wink. "By the way, thank you for the hot chocolate. I didn't think I'd like it, but the subtle minty flavor is delicious."

"You're welcome," his friend beamed.

Alexandra took a long sip of the steaming brew, cheeks reddened at his answer.

"You were right," she admitted, playing with the edge of her paper napkin.

"Right about what?" he asked then took a sip of his room temperature beverage.

"Macintosh grabbed my butt, the big jerk," she huffed, and her cheeks heated again. "I still can't believe he did that. He's meant to be a professional. We weren't at a nightclub. We were having a business meeting for goodness sakes."

"Huh," he snorted, trying to hide a sudden pang of jealousy. "Did you smack him?"

*Please say you smacked him… hard!*

To his disappointment she shook her head no.

"If he ever tries that again, I give you permission to slap the shit out of him," Roman advised, completely serious.

"I'll remember your advice," Alexandra agreed with a snicker then took a long sip of the still steaming brew. "If we were still in Florida, I'd be wearing shorts and a t-shirt right now. Nights like this, don't you miss the year-round warmth of Clearwater?"

Immediately Roman grimaced.

"I hated those hot summers in Florida," he shook his head as flashbacks of the temperature made him groan. "The terrible humidity, the freakishly-sized mosquitoes—"

"—the incredible theme parks with the best turkey legs on the planet, the friendly people, the gorgeous white sandy beaches," she reminded, taking another sip. "I thought you loved it there."

"The only thing I ever liked about Florida was you." He immediately straightened at the words that rushed out of his mouth of their own accord. The truth was he was glad they did. Relieved actually.

"Wow!" Alexandra mumbled shyly, watching him with a cautious glare. "I didn't expect you to say that."

Roman just sat motionless hoping for a twister to pick him up and transport him to anywhere but there. He saw that in a movie once and thought it was the coolest thing ever. Now that he was older, it probably wouldn't be so great.

After a very long pause, she finally broke the silence.

"I think that's the sweetest thing you've ever said to me," she grinned.

"Don't get a swelled head," her employer sheepishly grinned too. "But it's true."

"Really?" A small smile played at the corners of her mouth.

"It's true." He nodded. "I tolerated it because my parents decided to move from Manhattan to Clearwater to be near my grandparents when they retired. Having you as a friend made it bearable."

"I see," she whispered at a loss for words.

"Why haven't you ever dated?" Roman asked on a whim.

Stunned by his direct question, her eyes widened right before her cheeks turned a deep shade of crimson.

"I'm not trying to be humorous," he added frankly. "I mean, you're intelligent, beautiful, and funny. I don't understand how you could be single for so long."

# Four Past Midnight

She sat staring at him for a moment.

"You really think I'm *beautiful?*"

Reaching across the table, he rested his hand on hers.

"Yes really." His heart clenched in his chest at their innocent contact. "I'm still waiting for an answer."

"I don't know," Alexandra sighed. "I've liked different guys throughout the years, but I always felt awkward around them. I never knew what to say or how to act. Dating seemed more like a chore than fun."

"I never realized you felt that way," Roman admitted, suddenly feeling sorry for her.

"Do you think I'm odd?" she asked nervously.

"No, I think you're amazing," he immediately responded, adamantly shaking his head.

"I never saw that coming either," she announced with a dazzling smile.

"Anyway, I'd dreamt of attending Columbia since I was ten when my elementary school took a field trip to the campus." He paused. "I've told you this story before."

She shook her head no.

"I thought I had."

He knew he had. Somehow, he knew, and he knew what was coming next if he didn't change their path.

"That's neat you knew from such a young age you wanted to be in journalism like Woodward and Bernstein," Alexandra complimented with all sincerity.

A glazed look came over his rugged features.

"Not only that but seeing all of those hot chicks walking around in tight shorts and body-hugging tops, gotta love it!"

"You are such a pig!" She threw the crumpled paper napkin at his head, hitting him between his eyebrows.

"Seriously, though," Roman countered, taking her slender hands in his once again, enjoying the way they fit together. "You are the most important person in my life and I'm grateful to be able to call you my best friend, and I wouldn't have met you if my parents hadn't moved."

Suspiciously, her eyes narrowed, and a frown replaced her smile.

"You are acting so weird today," the woman declared. "It's freaking me out, a lot."

"Let's get outta here, 'Woodward'." He stood and helped her put on her raincoat.

Disappointment tugged at her.

"Don't you want to hang out a little more?" she suggested, enjoying their time together. "The rain might stop soon."

"No, the rain's not going to stop," Roman studied the gray sky outside. "We should leave now before it gets worse."

"Okay, Bernstein," she retorted with a chuckle.

# Four Past Midnight

As agreed, Alexandra paid the check, bought a chocolate chip muffin for later, and then they both made their way to the front entrance. It always stunned her that New York City streets were still bustling with people so late at night, natives and tourists alike. People of all shapes, sizes, and colors resembled migrating herds as they took in all the city had to offer. It was a pretty amazing sight to see.

"Wait." Roman tugged her sleeve, stopping her in midstride. "I'm not in the mood to walk in this weather. Let's take the subway."

"Why?" Alexandra wondered aloud.

"That intersection is really dangerous," he justified, shrugging his shoulders.

Instead, they made their way in the opposite direction, totally bypassing the corner and the crosswalk.

"You can't be too safe crossing the street in the big city, especially in downtown Manhattan where the cabbies are notoriously fast drivers."

"Whatever you say, boss." She watched him curiously. "Your stop is before mine. I don't want to ride the subway alone this late at night."

"It's okay," Roman calmly soothed. "I'll ride home with you, and then double back."

"That's ridiculous and a lot of traveling on your part," she lectured as if she were his mother.

"I don't mind," her childhood friend made his case. "I have to make a quick stop at my apartment to check on Bruno, but I promise it'll be quick."

"Sure, but this makes no sense," she half-heartedly agreed even though a sulk replaced her smile. "You're acting so peculiarly."

"What time is it?" Roman asked ignoring her last comment. The rain pounding against the synthetic, black material of his umbrella made it difficult to hear.

Alexandra pushed the sleeve of her raincoat up a tad to glance at the face of the gold wristwatch she wore.

"It's eleven thirty-five," she replied, readjusting her sleeve once again. She heard him let out a long, slow breath. "Are you in a hurry to get home to Bruno?"

She giggled as they walked to the subway entrance only a few feet away from the café.

"Ha! Ha!" Roman threw his dark locks back in a mocking laugh, suddenly righting himself and giving her one of his patented scowls.

"If you weren't my best friend, I'd kick your ass," she threatened, wondering if she could take him in a fight.

He tried to glare menacingly at her, but when she stuck out her tongue and crossed her eyes, he couldn't contain the peal of laughter that escaped his chest. The sound of him laughing only made her giggle more.

"How is Bruno? I haven't seen him in a while."

"Bruno thinks he's the owner and I'm the pet," he mused, adjusting the umbrella over her head.

"That's what I thought," she teased as Roman returned her playful scowl.

"Sometimes I feel a little jealous of the four-legged ball of fur," Alexandra admitted unashamed. "I wish you would pay me as much attention as you do Bruno."

One brow arched at her statement.

"I didn't know you felt that way," he responded with confusion.

"Forget about it," his partner in crime and loyal confidant brushed his comment aside, staring straight ahead. "What's on the agenda for tomorrow?"

Roman did not reply, only remained lost in his own thoughts.

Studying his current demeanor, she added, "Maybe I'll get another important lead to follow-up on."

"Maybe, but I wouldn't hold my breath. You know how fickle the owner of the paper is," Roman admonished, shaking his slightly, overly long, jet black locks. "But you never know, stranger things have happened."

With that said her lips thinned into a harsh line as she considered her response.

"I admit I'm not the best reporter at the office, but I'm not the worst either. I definitely know I'm better than Stan. The man can't even string two sentences together yet alone construct an entire cohesive article." Her eyes narrowed. "Why does he always get such great stories to research?"

"Stan is Sylvia's brother-in-law." Roman sighed. She started to protest, but he continued. "Unfortunately, nepotism is still alive and kicking."

"I guess so, but you are the editor don't you have the final say about who gets what assignments?"

Roman gave her a chastising stare.

"Fine, I won't mention it again."

"You can always seduce me into giving you the best stories," he teased, trying to get a reaction from her, which he did.

*"What?!"* The volume of her voice rose, and her cheeks heated. "Sexual harassment. That's how it starts. First, you're asking me to fetch coffee. Next, you'll want hanky-panky in the supply closet."

"That sounds reasonable to me," Roman's voice increased too then he reminded playfully, "You seem to be forgetting that *I* fetch *you* coffee."

"Oh, yeah," she chuckled, trying to contain her amusement. "I had the weirdest dream the other day about my hamster. Do you remember him?"

"Mr. Fuzzy, poor thing," Roman frowned. "How he managed to survive for three months with you as his owner is miraculous."

"That's not an accurate statement," the insulted Alexandra huffed, sidestepping a wide puddle.

"'Not an accurate statement'." He cringed. "You're joking right?"

The woman simply glared at him; her lips pressed tightly together.

## Four Past Midnight

"Why was Mr. Fuzzy's death my fault?" Alexandra snapped brusquely.

"You over fed him, and he died!" Roman reminded with wild open-handed gestures.

"I didn't make him eat all of those food pellets!" she snapped. "I think he might have had an eating disorder. I've heard on the news about pet stores selling defective animals. *Google* it if you don't believe me."

"That's the most insane thing you've ever said," he rebuked her hypothesis.

"Forget I said it," she mumbled below her breath. "I'm older now, wiser..."

There was only silence as he studied her.

She thought he was finished when he suddenly added, "What about, Izzy, the pet lizard you had in college?"

Brown eyes widened in horror as she exclaimed, "That carnivorous reptile attacked me! It grabbed onto my finger with its mouth and wouldn't let go!"

She contorted her hands in an attack position.

"I dropped it on the floor not realizing my bedroom window was open and the damn thing ran away."

"A deadly attack lizard?" he scoffed, making her feel like a complete moron.

"Don't laugh," she snorted. "They're distant relatives to the Komodo dragons."

His smirk disappeared.

"You are insane," he admonished with amusement.

"You've made your point," she finally admitted. "I guess a pet wouldn't be a good idea, now that I've reexamined my past track record."

A soft sigh escaped her.

"Thanks for reminding me of my pet failures, boss," her tone dripped with sarcasm, which she didn't bother to hide.

"No problem." Emerald eyes sparkled good-naturedly. "Anytime."

# V

Roughly ten minutes later, they were at his apartment, greeted by an extremely excited Bruno. The dog eagerly ran around their feet wagging his tail and licking their hands. Alexandra scratched behind his ears and under his chin. She laughed when he rolled over onto his back and offered up his spotted belly for a rub.

"You're so much cuter than your owner," she announced, grinning when Roman swatted her mischievously on the arm.

"I'm cuter than a dog," he informed jokingly, smacking her a bit harder on the shoulder.

"Watch it," she jibed, swatting him back, but he moved quickly, and she accidentally slapped his buttocks.

His eyes widened with amusement.

"Did you just grab my ass?" he asked with a saucy grin.

"*No!*" her words morphed into a squeak and her cheeks heated. "It was an accident!"

"Sure, it was." He watched her curiously, his tongue darting out to moisten his bottom lip. "You grabbed my ass without permission."

"I'm sorry," she apologized.

"Oh! My!" he sang. "How the tables have turned."

Roman's eyes sparkled teasingly.

"Who's the pervert now, Miss Martin?"

Feeling lucky, he strode toward her temporarily forgetting about Bruno, who sat on his hind legs enjoying the show.

Alexandra's body stiffened as he stalked her, a mischievous gleam in his eyes.

"Roman," she warned, taking a step back. "What are you doing?"

Raising his hands, he wiggled his fingers.

"No!" she advised again, only louder. "Do not tickle me."

Then she stepped back.

"I hate it when you do that, Roman."

"All's fair," he educated, taking another step forward.

His much longer strides rapidly closing the distance between them.

"It's either this or write you up for—" he thought for a few seconds before finishing, "—sexual harassment."

"Be serious," Alexandra growled, circling the sofa and heading back to the foyer.

"I am," he winked. "Your punishment will be this."

He wiggled his digits again.

# Four Past Midnight

Alexandra hated to be tickled. Hated it with a passion. She had once told him the story of when her Aunt Jenna tickled her at her sixth birthday party, and she lost control of her bladder—in front of everyone! Since then, she promised to slug anyone who tried to tickle her. He tickled her right after she told him about the *'incident'* and true to her word, she punched him straight in the eye. Embarrassed to be assaulted by a girl, he went to school the next day and told his buddies that he was rescuing a drowning puppy from a lake and the panicking pooch kicked him in the face causing the blackeye. Yup! That was the tale he told, and he hoped he would take it to the grave.

Instinctively, she turned to run, but he grabbed her around the waist and hauled her against him.

"Don't tickle me!" she reiterated, breath escaping in choppy pants. Inhaling, her lungs filled with the faint scent of Roman's cologne and his natural essence. He smelled divine.

"There must be proper punishment," he growled, eyes dilated, a heated gaze locked on her mouth.

"I have a get out of jail free pass," she whispered as his head descended.

Whispering back, he reminded, "This isn't Monopoly."

With that said, Roman's lips found hers. Soft, fleeting pecks intermingled with barely-there brushes taunted her.

"What are you doing?" Alexandra gulped for breath after he pulled away, but his hands still gently cupped her face.

"I don't know," he admitted, using his thumbs to trace the contours of her face. "I've wanted to kiss you all day."

Her heart pounded loudly in her ears.

"You have?" she muttered, her head spinning.

"Uh-huh," he sighed, mouth returning, harder and needier. His tongue pushed against her lips demanding entry. On a surprised gasp, she opened and was instantly assaulted by Roman's wickedly talented muscle. Boldly, he explored every corner, licking, nipping and sucking. If he didn't stop soon, there would be no telling what would happen next.

Fighting the need to let him take her, she pushed against his chest.

"Roman, please, stop."

"Why?" he pleaded, moving to her neck where he lavished the area with sultry licks and needy nips. "Haven't you ever wondered what it would be like between us?"

His hands drifted from her face to her nipped-in waist.

Arching her neck to give him better access, she asked, "Wonder about what?"

"*Sex*... how it would be between us," he coerced, securing his hold around her waist. His mouth continued its explorations.

His proclamation brought her back to her senses.

"Stop."

"Give me one good reason why we should stop," he stated, lowering his hands to cup her ass.

Naturally, her body tensed.

# Four Past Midnight

"Because we're best friends and I don't want sex to ruin what we have."

As if a bucket of cold water had been poured over his head, he immediately paused.

"I'm sorry," he apologized, voice barely audible. "I don't know what's wrong with me today."

"I-it's okay." She stared at him wanting to continue, but knowing it was a bad idea. They had been best friends for so long she didn't want to mess up their relationship.

Slowly, he released her and walked back to the foyer where Bruno still sat patiently. In a daze, Roman grabbed the leash and a small plastic bag.

"I have to take him out," the disappointed man told his equally stunned friend. "Do you mind coming with me?"

"I don't mind," Alexandra replied, voice hardly a whisper.

Sadly, her brain was still confused by their kiss; perhaps the cool night air would weaken her desire.

Without a word, they made their way to the sidewalk in front of Roman's apartment building. The rain was now coming down in sheets and they could barely see two feet in front of where they walked. Needless to say, it was difficult convincing Bruno to do his business.

"C'mon Bruno, make it fast," he firmly requested, but to his dismay, Bruno only watched him like he had lost his mind, refusing to move. "He'll go if I take him into the park. Wait here. I'll be right back."

"Okay, take the umbrella," she said, handing him the much-needed device. "My hood keeps me nice and dry."

"Yeah, but it's ugly." He smirked.

"It is not ugly," she huffed, words filled with indignation and mirth, easing the tension between them.

"If you say so," he chuckled before looking both ways then crossing the street with his disgruntled dog, not bothering to wait for the signal to turn. Then as luck would have it, a sudden gust of wind came out of nowhere and ripped the umbrella out of his hand into the middle of the road.

"Don't worry, I got it!"

Roman heard Alexandra call out above the sound of the deluge that fell from the dark sky. Simultaneously, he glanced back in time to see the crosswalk signal change to green as Alexandra made a move, but before he could get her attention she stepped off of the sidewalk into the road. At that exact moment, the loud sound of tires screeching filled the night, as the same speeding taxi ran through the red light just as she attempted to cross the street. The sound faded quickly as the driver raced away.

"*No!*" he screamed, sprinting in her direction. "*Alexandra!* This can't be fucking happening again!"

Frantically he looked around; trying to find Alexandra, a renewed sense of dread showing its ugly head. This time there was no blonde woman to his left to let out a blood curdling scream. Instead, the scream came from him. Alexandra's bright yellow rain jacket lay over twenty feet away near a newsstand. A sick feeling settled into his bones.

On instinct, he raced toward her, forgetting Bruno was running to keep up with him. As fast as his legs could go, he ran. Ran toward that damn yellow jacket, horror stealing his breath at the sight he found on the relatively clean street in front of his apartment building.

"*Alexandra!*" He yelled his friend's name, the pained sound muffled by the worsening weather.

A burly man standing on the corner ran over to help.

"Why does this keep happening?" he asked her limp form, hoping she would open her baby browns and answer.

"I called 911!" the man informed breathlessly. "They're on their way! I got that asshole's license plate number too, the fuckin' bastard!"

"Alexandra! Dear God! *No!*" He held her in one hand and Bruno's leash in the other. "*Alexandra! No! No!*"

*Motherfucker!*

He didn't know how long he had sat there. Now, the rain was just a drizzle and the sky had started to clear as he sat rocking her limp form in his trembling arms. George, the doorman of his building, was kind enough to take Bruno back to his apartment.

*Why did this keep happening?*

None of this made any sense!

The ten minutes it took for the paramedics to arrive seemed like an eternity, and by that time, they had to pry him off of her.

"Sir, you need to let go of her," a gruff male voice commanded close to his ear.

That only made him hug her tighter, ignoring the man completely as despair threatened to completely consume him.

"Open your eyes. Open your eyes and talk to me," Roman ordered, shaking her gently. "Call me a slave driver. Call me a womanizer. Call me something… anything."

The need to touch her overwhelmed him.

"Sir, you're gonna have to let go of her," the EMT stated impatiently. "We need to get her to the hospital."

"I'm not letting her go alone. I'm riding in the ambulance with her." His expression dared the guy to refuse.

The EMT's eyes narrowed as he asked, "Are you two related?"

"Yes, I'm her brother," he lied, holding his breath.

The other man studied him, and seeing his anguish gave in to his demand.

"Then you can ride in the back of the ambulance with her."

"Thanks," Roman whispered, finally releasing Alexandra's cold, wet body to the EMT.

Immediately, the two paramedics took her from him and placed her on a stretcher.

"Sir, we've got a lot of medical equipment inside: monitors, IV's, syringes, antiseptics, and a bunch of supplies. It's gonna be a tight squeeze," the EMT explained as they carried her to the ambulance.

Roman nodded in acknowledgement.

"Also, it smells medicinal: harsh and sterile. I'm used to it, but sometimes it can make first timers feel a bit nauseous."

"I'll be fine," Roman answered unemotionally, which surprised him since he was being flooded with every emotion under the sun. "I have a strong stomach."

This had happened before. Not in the exact same way, but it happened. This time, he was positive of it.

*What kind of sick shit was he going through?!*

"Do you think she's gonna be okay, Tom?" he questioned, glancing at the man's name badge.

The emergency technician had just finished attaching Alexandra's IV line, securing her neck brace, and was now checking her vital statistics. Just like the female EMT, Tom was doing everything by the book. Sadly, Roman knew that none of it mattered because it would end the same.

Tom paled.

"I'm not a doctor, Sir, but she's young and healthy." The man swallowed hard before adding, "All we can do is hope for the best."

"She's gonna be fine." Roman took her hand again. "Do you hear me, Sunshine? You're gonna be fine."

The bile rising in his throat reminded him otherwise.

Just as before, the ten-minute ride to the hospital was the longest ten minutes of his life. Anxiety filled him as the vehicle pulled into the emergency entrance and parked. Tensely, he followed the gurney that carried Alexandra until a nurse stopped him and directed him to the waiting room.

Impatiently, he waited in the generically decorated waiting area, pacing nervously until he thought he might have worn a path in the cheap linoleum. All the while silently mumbling a prayer… something he hadn't done since the previous night. The clock on the wall ticking loudly reminded of what was about to happen. Again.

Right on time, a man's voice called from the doorway.

"Mr. Giordano?" His green scrubs indicated who he was, although Roman would never forget his face.

"Yes, that's me." His stomach lurched at the doctor's uneasy manner. "Go ahead, say it. I already know."

The doctor looked down at his chart.

"I'm sorry, but Miss Martin had a coronary attack upon arrival."

*"God!"* he groaned.

At his outburst, Dr. Reed's body stiffened.

# Four Past Midnight

"I'm truly sorry, but we did everything we could."

"I'm sure you did," he replied numbly, and his body began to shake uncontrollably.

Clearing his throat the doctor added, "We did CPR and had to use the defibrillator several times, but there was a lot of hemorrhaging and severe brain swelling. I'm so sorry for your loss."

Roman felt the room shift below his feet before realizing he had stumbled onto his knees. The doctor was shouting for a wheelchair and a nurse as he lay immobile on the cold hospital floor, listening to the chaos around him, but numb to it all.

"I need some help over here, Nurse Marshall!" Dr. Reed shouted over his shoulder. It was the last thing he heard before the room went black.

Exactly as Roman remembered, he woke on a gurney near the nurse's station across from the waiting room. The usual small carton of orange juice waited for him; however, this time there was no cookie. Slowly, he looked around in confusion, the surreal nature of what continued to happen scratched at his soul like a wild beast.

Quickly, he drank all of the juice hoping it would give him the strength to stand, and after a few minutes, he was finally able to even though his legs felt weak and wobbly. Like a bass drum being played in his head, his temples throbbed as he followed his previous path toward the restricted section of the hospital.

"I'm responsible, damn it!" he mumbled as the accident replayed in his mind. "She'd still be alive if I hadn't offered her the reporter's job at the newspaper. She would be safe in Clearwater teaching at Chesterfield High School's English department. She'd be alive and I'd still have my best friend."

Tears were streaming down his face now.

"I'll fix it," he mumbled to himself, hands grasped tightly, knuckles turning white from the pressure. "No matter what it takes I'll fix it. I'll get it right the next time. I'll change everything about the day."

A commotion from the emergency room entrance caught his attention as another patient was rushed to an empty examination room. His heart clenched in his chest as he watched the chaotic scene. Alexandra's lifeless body flashed over and over in his mind as he remembered her being wheeled into a similar room.

"*Dr. Reed you're needed in emergency exam room two, STAT!*" The voice on the intercom system sounded overhead.

Of their own accord, salty rivulets of tears flowed down his face, but he didn't care who saw. Brushing them away angrily, he began his well-known path through the quiet hospital hallways. The same third-shift nurse, who had assisted Dr. Reed when he fell in the waiting room, saw him. Her furrowed brow made him feel even worse.

Right on cue, the kind voice of Nurse Marshall called out to him.

"Excuse me, Sir," she said, handing him a cup of hot coffee from a nearby dispenser. "You shouldn't be wandering around this area. It's restricted."

# Four Past Midnight

Looking up he noticed the familiar sign on the door stating, *'Employees Only'*.

"I know," he mumbled. "I'm sorry."

Understanding his anguish, her expression softened.

"Do you want me to call you a cab?"

He shook his head.

"I'm surprised you're still here," the nurse confessed. "You should head home. You need to rest."

"I know, but I can't go home," Roman admitted, holding back another onslaught of tears. "I don't want to be alone. Not yet."

The nurse's voice lowered before she asked, "The young lady who passed away, was she your girlfriend?"

His heart clenched.

"No, she was my best friend," Roman divulged, the reality hitting home. "Actually, she was my only *real* friend. I've known her since the ninth grade. I don't know what I'm going to do without her."

Nurse Marshall rested a comforting hand on his shoulder.

"I see," she spoke softly as if he was a timid animal. "I'm so sorry for your loss."

"Thanks."

He really hated that phrase. One day he'd find the person who first said it and kick the shit out of him.

"Listen, why don't you go up to the chapel?"

"It's on the third floor, isn't it?" he recalled.

"Yes, it's nice and quiet there," the nurse encouraged. "Saying a prayer might help you feel better. Sometimes when things aren't going my way, I like to stop in and light a candle or two and put things into perspective. It's a relatively small thing to do, but it always makes me feel better."

Roman nodded his agreement as he followed the nurse to the small chapel.

"Thank you, Nurse Marshall."

"How do you know my name?" Both of her brows hitched in confusion.

"Isn't that what Dr. Reed called you downstairs in the waiting room?" he lied so she wouldn't freak out.

"Yes, of course." The nurse seemed pensive. "I am truly sorry about what happened to your friend."

"I appreciate you saying that."

"Have you ever had one of those nights where it feels like everything has happened before?" the woman asked, totally serious.

"Yes, I have," he mumbled. "In fact, I know I've spoken with you before."

"Really?" she asked, body tensing. "We've met?"

"We have, but it's alright if you don't remember me. It was only briefly."

# Four Past Midnight

He smiled and her bright blue eyes sparkled like sapphires as she smiled back. The kindness in her face made him feel safe.

"Sorry," Nurse Marshall apologized, cheeks reddening. "I'm usually great at remembering people. I must be getting old."

"No worries," Roman gave a small smile. "Thank you again."

"You are more than welcome." She gave a quick wink, smiled and then walked away, leaving him alone with his misery.

Reluctantly, he entered the small room. He had seen the soft muted color scheme of the chapel before, and it eased his apprehension a bit knowing what to expect. The charming Spanish-style decor would have impressed him if it was in another place and another time, but now it made him feel desperate. Desperate to stop whatever it was that kept happening to him… to Alexandra.

There was no doubt he had done all of this before. He had prayed, often during the past few nights, but he still felt hollow inside. Now, he regretted abandoning his faith all of those years ago. Maybe he was being punished.

As usual, there was no one else in the small room. By habit he chose a pew near the front, the one he always sat in near the lit candles. The heat radiating off of them reminded him that he was still damp from the rain. With heavy limbs, he removed his jacket and laid the garment over the back of the pew to dry.

"How do I stop this madness?" he asked the crucifix secured to the front wall of the chapel. At least it didn't answer back. His tears flowed again, and he let them. Let them run down his face until his eyes burned from it, but this time he had hope. Hope that he'd have another chance to save her.

Finally, he knelt and closed his eyes. The silence filling him with dread at the thought it was about to start all over again.

"Heavenly Father, I've prayed every night since this crazy loop started and it always resets. How do I get this nightmare to end? How do I save Alexandra?"

# VI

*Beep! Beep! Beep!*

"Today is going to be different!" Roman slowly opened his eyes, a thin layer of sweat covering his body making him shiver even though the room itself was slightly warm.

The alarm clock on the nearby nightstand blared, reminding him of his early meeting at the newspaper with Alexandra.

*Alexandra!*

Suddenly he, bolted into a seated position and tried to stand, but he was drenched, and his wet legs were wrapped in the sheets like a burrito. The material wound so tightly that he fell off of the bed and landed in a heap on the shag carpet. Red-rimmed eyes burned as if he hadn't slept at all.

*He knew exactly what day it was.*

Glancing at the clock again, it confirmed it was Tuesday, October 22.

"This is real. It's *not* just a nightmare," he mumbled to Bruno who was watching him from the foot of his king-sized bed. The dog looked down at where he was sprawled on the floor and gave a sad whimper.

Then he stilled. Bombarded with overwhelming certainty, this had happened previously. Several times in fact. The realization made his heart clench inside of his chest, but he soldiered on.

Still in a sleep-drunk haze, he pulled himself up to a standing position, his breathing shallow and choppy. Rapidly, he jogged to the ensuite bathroom and completed his morning ritual of showering, shaving, brushing his teeth, and styling his hair in only ten minutes.

Standing inside of his walk-in closet, he already knew which suit, shirt, and tie he *didn't* want to wear, his black Armani suit, pale blue button-down dress shirt, and a blue, black, and gray tie with geometric shapes on it. Instead, he chose his gray and white pin-stripe suit, white button-down dress shirt, sans tie, and his black *Jimmy Choo* shoes.

Unwillingly, his thoughts drifted to the nightmare that plagued his sleep. The one he was sure wasn't a nightmare at all, but some sort of supernatural time loop he was stuck in.

*Dear God!*

He sounded insane.

A grimace marred his face when he remembered his best friend bleeding in his arms. The pungent scent of the city mixed with Alexandra's softly scented *Chanel* perfume suddenly attacked his mind. He held on to that thought and went to get dressed and was determined not to let it happen again.

On his way to the full-length mirror behind his bedroom door, he stopped, grabbed his cell phone, and speed dialed Alexandra. The need to hear her voice clawing away inside of him like a beast trapped in a cage. The line rang and she picked up on the third ring.

# Four Past Midnight

"Hello?" her voice raspy and sounding very sexy.

"Good morning, Sunshine!" he greeted warmly.

There was a brief pause before she muttered, "Roman? Why are you calling me at 6:55 in the morning? I still have five minutes to sleep."

Grateful to spend another day with her, he chuckled.

"No, you don't," Roman scoffed. "If you go back to sleep now, you'll be off of your schedule, and you know how pissy you are when that happens."

She yawned before saying, "You know me so well."

"Yes… yes, I do."

There was silence once more, making him worry.

"Alexandra? Alexandra, get your ass outta bed. Right the hell now."

"Jeez! Okay, alright. I'm up you big slave driver," her annoyance unmasked.

"I love it when you call me a slave driver," he chuckled. "It makes me feel important."

"I'm hanging up on you now," she yawned again. "I have to turn on my coffeemaker. You know how I am if I don't get that cup-a-Joe first thing in the morning."

He hated to be the bearer of bad news, but, "Alexandra?"

"Yeah?" she responded sleepily.

"Don't bother making coffee," he broke the bad news. "Your cheap coffee machine is broken. I'm gonna get you a mocha latte from the Sweetshop Café."

"It can't be broken," Alexandra groaned with frustration. "I bought it last week, but you can still buy me a latte."

"I will," he grinned widely, knowing she couldn't see his sentimental expression.

"I love their coffee," her tone lightened. "I'll see you soon."

"Wait! Wait!" he yelled before she could hang up.

"What now?" she sighed.

"It's rainy out. It's only a drizzle right now, but the meteorologist said it's gonna get worse as the day goes on."

"Great!" sarcasm laced her word.

"Sucks right?" he agreed, needing to hear her lovely voice for a few more minutes.

"Sure does," the still groggy female yawned for the third time. "But I've got that new rain jacket I bought last week—"

"No! Do not wear that ugly piece of plastic," he ordered, never wanting to see the hideous thing again. "Use your umbrella and I'll meet you at work."

"No problem, but to clarify… my jacket is not ugly."

"Yes, it is and you're forbidden to wear it ever again," he retorted, laughing.

# Four Past Midnight

"Do you have to be so damn rude this early in the morning?" Alexandra countered.

"Yes… yes, I do." He began to hang up when something else came to mind. "Alexandra, wait!"

"I'm gonna kill you, Roman," she threatened.

"Sorry, I forgot to ask you one more thing."

"What is it?"

He could imagine her eyes rolling.

"Do you still have that royal blue dress you wore to the office banquet last month?"

"Why?" her voice dripped with suspicion.

"Could you wear that today instead of the black pencil skirt with the plumb blouse?"

"I thought you said that color was nice on me, brought out the color of my eyes or some such nonsense. Now you're saying you don't like it."

*Why was she so exasperating?*

Alexandra was driving him crazy, literally.

"You look great in that outfit, but you wear it all of the time," he blurted. "Choose something else. It doesn't have to be that dress, alright?"

"For your information, I haven't worn that outfit in a month," she informed smugly.

There was a brief pause.

"But if you insist, I'll find something else to wear today."

"Terrific!" he hesitated. "And do something with your hair."

"You are such an asshole!" the woman bellowed into the device. "What's wrong with my hair?"

"Sorry, can't... hear... you. We've got... a... bad connection..." he lied, making crackling sounds with his mouth.

"Roman, I'm gonna kick your ass when I see you—"

Before she could call him another unbecoming name, he hung up, chuckling to himself the entire time.

The morning was progressing fairly well for Alexandra.

*It was great, actually.*

First, the alarm clock she bought for a steal of three dollars never sounded, which would have made her late, but because of Roman's unexpected early morning phone call she was almost twenty minutes ahead of schedule. This pleased her since she'd never been late for work in her entire life. Never. It bothered her to think she might not have made it into the office before Roman. She was OCD in that respect.

Second, the hot water system of her one-hundred-year-old apartment building had been on the fritz all last week. Naturally, she thought she'd have to take a shower in frigid water. The possibility of icicles forming on the tip of her nose didn't appeal to her. However, Mr. Endicott, the building superintendent, had already been harassed by several other tenants earlier that morning and had fixed the problem, according to nosey Mrs. Walters in apartment six-B. Instead, she was able to enjoy a nice hot shower.

Next, her brand-new coffeemaker that she purchased at a going out of business sale dripped out only five drops of brownish-gray liquid then sputtered, clanked and refused to work. Thirty dollars down the proverbial drain, but Roman was getting her coffee anyway, so it wasn't a big deal. And not only coffee, but her favorite. Giddy with joy, she grinned to herself.

And if that wasn't good enough, she searched the back of her closet for the royal blue dress to wear for her early meeting with Roman at the office and found a brand-new black sheath dress. The garment had never been worn and still sported the sales tags. Her mother had sent her the dress in case she needed something nice to wear for an important meeting or convention or something along those same lines. It was perfect!

Roman always looked so fashionable in his expensive, imported suits that hugged his well-chiseled body in all the right places. His dress shirts always perfectly pressed and matched his tie. The three-hundred-dollar designer shoes didn't hurt either. For the life of her, she never understood why the man had to buy such expensive footwear.

Methodically, Alexandra took her time getting ready, primping and shaving, buffing and applying lotion. She even took a few extra minutes to shape her eyebrows. It had been a long time and she was thankful they hadn't turned into a unibrow. The idea made her giggle.

Next was her hair, a task in itself; however, determination fueled her movements as she searched under her sink until she found her anti-frizz solution and styling gel. The bottles hadn't even been opened yet. Meticulously, she applied the styling products, blew dried and flat ironed her hair and was surprised they worked. Her tresses, which normally would be difficult on a day like today, the humidity causing it to expand and frizz until she resembled a French poodle, actually stayed in soft layers around her face.

After almost ten minutes of doing this annoying process, she consulted the mirror and smiled. She looked more than presentable if she said so herself. Her chest puffed out with feminine pride.

Cautiously, she got dressed taking great care not to mess-up her hair. The simple yet elegant sheath dress hugged her curves in all of the right places, giving the illusion of two inches more cleavage. An enthusiastic fist punch echoed her delight as she silently thanked her mom for having excellent taste.

Roman would *definitely* approve.

She had to admit, choosing her black pencil skirt and plumb button-down silk blouse would have enhanced her complexion and made her chocolate, brown eyes look more exotic, but this dress made her look sexy, yet professional. A pair of simple black flats completed the outfit since she was much too clumsy to wear high heels.

At last, with a steady hand she applied eyeliner and mascara which brought out the rich brown of her irises and a thin layer of nude lip gloss that made her naturally full lips seem even fuller. As usual, her complexion was acceptable. She'd never needed to wear concealer or foundation since she'd been blessed with clear, perfect skin. In her opinion, it was her one saving grace. She smiled at her reflection. It wasn't *Covergirl* perfection, but it wasn't *Jabba the Hutt* either.

# Four Past Midnight

Glancing at the clock one more time, she grinned. Ready in only thirty minutes. She was sure to beat Mr. GQ to the office. It was going to be a good day.

# VII

"Good morning, Sun—" Roman halted in midsentence, which was *not* his normal greeting. Neither was the way he stared at her, emerald eyes raking her from head to toe and then back again. The blatant heat contained there caused her upper lip to perspire.

"What do you think?" Alexandra inquired, striking a pose and puckering her lips.

*"Huh?"* The man blinked, but still stood there with his mouth open.

"You didn't finish your greeting or tell me if you like what I'm wearing," her hands perched on her hips.

"Huh." A complete sentence eluded him. Shaking his head in an attempt to clear the lust-filled thoughts accosting his brain he managed a dumbfounded, "What?"

"Ever since the ninth grade you've always said, 'Good morning, Sunshine,'" she mimicked in her best baritone. "Always."

"I'm sorry." He still stared with his mouth open. "You caught me off guard."

"What do you think?" She gave a graceful twirl. "I know you asked me to wear the blue dress, but I—"

# Four Past Midnight

"You're perfect!" Roman exclaimed then ran his index finger over his bottom lip to make sure there wasn't any drool. Alexandra looked good enough to eat, and he had no problem doing just that. "I think you look amazing, like a supermodel."

She grinned, his compliment adding to her self-confidence. Surprisingly, he wasn't wearing his well-tailored, black Armani suit, which he usually did on Thursdays.

"You look terrific as well," she flattered, examining his stylish gray suit, but something was off. "You're not wearing a tie today?"

That was it.

"I thought I'd try a more casual look," he explained dismissively.

"I like it." Her words made him blush and his perfect smile brightened her sunny disposition even more on this rainy autumn day.

"I'm glad you do," he grinned.

The sincerity in his voice did strange things to her nether regions and she began to shift uneasily on the office chair.

"Now that all of those pleasantries are out of the way, where's my latte?"

Alexandra gazed up at him; eyes twinkled under the bright lighting. Her expression spoke volumes of how she felt. Hypnotic doe-eyes surrounded by long, thick, black lashes spread up and out like fans caught and held his attention.

And the dress. *Jeez, the dress.* Soft material clung to every subtle curve of her physique, hugging and molding to every dip, every rounded surface. It took every bit of self-control he possessed not to reach out and touch her.

"Roman?"

"Sorry, the dress keeps distracting me," he apologized with a wink.

"Stop it." She stared down at the growing stack of articles on her cluttered desk.

"I'm sorry, Sunshine," he leered, his tone sultry as well as unexpected.

Her shocked glare brought him back to earth. Roman chuckled, holding his hands up in surrender.

"I haven't given you your coffee yet." It wasn't a question.

Like a child, she pouted and shook her head in defeat.

"Here, I know you'll enjoy it," he stated with that air of confidence she'd always admired. "I picked up an extra-large, double sweet, double shot, mocha latte for you. Next time, I'll get you a different flavor."

Suddenly he stopped, looked around, and realized things were different now. She was different. They were different. It was a good start.

"What's wrong?" Alexandra watched him with a frown.

"Huh?"

"You? Are you alright?" she pressed him for an honest answer. "It's like you just zoned-out for a moment, and you haven't been acting like your usual self."

# Four Past Midnight

"Have you ever had that feeling you've done something before?" He shook his head, massaging his nape, the tense muscles bothering him.

"Explain," she urged.

"You know, when you do or say something, and it feels like you've already done it."

After a few seconds she answered.

"Ah, yeah... *déjà vu*. Sure, it happens to everyone."

"That's it," he said with a smirk. "Right now, our conversation feels like *déjà vu*."

"Beyonce has a song called *Déjà Vu*... thought you'd want to know," she added with a wave of her hand.

"Thanks for that meaningless bit of trivia," he chuckled under his breath.

She began waving her arms around in undulating waves.

"Have you ever thought maybe, all of this—"

"—is a lab on an alien space station where they are studying our human bodies so they can clone us." Roman interrupted as he arched his brows playfully, making her laugh out loud.

"I was just going to say that exact thing," she snorted.

"Were you?" He feigned innocence. "Great minds think alike."

"I guess." His silly counterpart made a funny face at him and stuck out her tongue.

"Remind me again. Why do I keep you around?" Roman teased.

"Because no one in their right mind will put up with you?"

"Probably," he scoffed.

She smiled then. A real smile that told him her day had just become even better all because of him. Alexandra couldn't help noticing the blush that stole over her best friend's face.

"Here, stop being a smart ass and drink your coffee."

Appreciatively, she took the disposable plastic travel cup from his hands.

"Thank you, boss," she acknowledged with a devilish wink.

The action made him blush again.

"You look especially handsome today, but then again you always do."

His eyes narrowed suspiciously at her comment.

"I mean... you always take the time to look your best, unlike me."

"Like I said before," Roman emphasized. "You look incredible this morning."

"Thank you." She blushed.

"That dress is hot!"

"Hot?!" she repeated, glancing down to confirm his claim. "I'll have to wear this dress more often."

# Four Past Midnight

"Okay, enough." Roman waved away her look of appreciation, getting back to the task at hand. "What have you got on the public utility story?"

With admiration, she watched him walk around the solid mahogany desk. Visions of him draping her over the sturdy piece of furniture and claiming her like a beast in heat made her temperature rise and her sex clench excitedly. Even with his puffy, red eyes he was still gorgeous: tall, golden, and powerful. The mere sight of him was enough to make her chest tighten and she rubbed her palm over her heart to ease the sensation.

*She had it bad.*

He cleared his throat to get her attention.

"Alexandra Maria Martin?"

"Huh?"

His forehead creased.

"Who's zoning out now? The public works story… how's it going?" he asked, even though he already knew her answer.

He leaned against the edge of her desk, long legs stretching out in front of him as he waited for her response. The intense look she gave him made his eyes narrow with suspicion.

"Why are you rubbing your chest like that?" His gaze glued to her movement. The idea of his hand taking its place made him grin.

She looked embarrassed for some reason.

"What did you say?"

"Are you alright?" Roman grilled, hoping she wasn't having a heart attack in this dream sequence. "You're rubbing your chest."

"Y-yes, my c-coffee went down the wrong way," the usually cool journalist stammered. "I'm okay. What was your question?"

"Public. Works. Story," he repeated each word slowly mocking her. If he did it in sign language, she'd kick his firmly, packed ass.

Steeling her nerves, she inhaled deeply.

"The one about the increase in prices for the third year in a row?"

He nodded.

"I've got a source at the public works department that's dying to spill the beans on his boss's misuse of funds. My confidential informant claims—"

Unexpectedly, he cut her off in midsentence saying.

"The extra money is allegedly being used for executive trips to Bora Bora and Botox shots for his wife."

Alexandra started to say something else, but was interrupted again.

"And yes—" he continued. "—I know how you feel about people injecting themselves with a poisonous toxin. It's not safe or healthy."

"Are you telepathic now, or something?" A huge frown marred her lovely face.

## Four Past Midnight

"Or something," Roman smirked, handing her a chocolate chip muffin from the brown paper bag he was carrying. She practically ripped the delicious treat from his extended hand.

"Mmm," she moaned, taking a large bite out of the miniature cake. Knowing not to bother her while she feasted on her favorite baked good, he waited patiently as she chewed and swallowed. "I love y… that you feed me."

Famished, she took another bite.

"Is it good?" he asked with a large grin. "It must be good."

*"Mmm-hmm,"* she added with a full mouth, making him laugh.

Again, he waited patiently until she finally spoke.

"I was planning on buying one of these this evening to take home with me," his companion confessed. "Maybe you are telepathic."

"I know that's not my problem," he mumbled, staring at her mouth, the simple act causing her to become self-conscious.

"Why are you staring?" She brushed her fingertips over her lips in case muffin crumbs had gathered there. "Is there something on my mouth?"

He desperately wanted to say he wished he was on her mouth, but he decided against it.

For some reason, he couldn't tear his gaze away from her soft, pouty lips.

*What the hell was he doing? Ogling his best friend's lips? He was going straight to hell.*

But the more he thought about it, the more he liked the idea of her... *of them*... together. And not just kissing like they had done the night before. No. What he wanted would require them naked and in his bed.

"You have a piece of—"

Without thought, he leaned over her desk, removing the small crumb with his slightly calloused thumb.

"There, all gone," he gazed longingly at her, thumb still lingering on her lips. "You really do look nice today. A more accurate description would be *beautiful*."

It took all of his willpower not to lean forward and kiss her.

Shocked, she stared at her messy desk.

"You've already mentioned that several times." Her voice cracked against her will.

Clearly, their proximity was making him overheated and horny.

"Have you spoken to Macintosh about the new stadium that's in the works?" She swallowed the lump in her throat and was about to reply when he answered for her.

"Don't tell me. You've got a meeting with him today." Roman paused, muffin still hovering near his mouth. "You're also having lunch with him."

"Is that a problem?" Alexandra's eyes narrowed.

"Yes, it is a problem," he boldly admitted.

He paused again, eyes going to the vee of her dress instead.

# Four Past Midnight

*Dear heaven!*

*He wanted so badly to bend forward and nestle his face in that cleavage!*

"How do you know what I am going to say or do? Tell me the truth or I'll slug you," his agitated friend threatened.

"I told you; this has all happened before," Roman's voice rose in volume. "I can't explain it, but it's true. Except now it's different."

"Please explain why I shouldn't have lunch with this man." Defiantly, her arms folded across her chest, blocking his view. "I'm waiting, Roman."

Not wanting to look like he was intimidated by her, he folded his arms across his chest in a defensive posture too.

"The guy's a total sleaze."

Alexandra mimicked his tone.

"Why do you think he's a sleaze?"

"I've heard from reliable sources he's hit on every woman in his department, married, single, and almost retired, anything in a skirt basically. I've also heard he's used his female contacts to procure favors and he treats women like sex objects instead of people. And at lunch he's gonna grab your ass," Roman rambled.

"He must be your long-lost brother," she teased impishly.

"I've never grabbed your ass," he announced gruffly. "Even though right now, looking the way you do, I really want to."

She threw her thick mane of ebony hair back, laughing until her eyes filled with unshed tears.

"Did you just—"

"That's not what I meant. However, your ass is looking really fine today," he interjected, stopping when she shot him a shocked stare.

"I see," she glared.

"I may be a lot of things, but I don't grope women unless they want me to," Roman corrected, sticking his foot in his mouth. "I also don't believe in using women."

"You don't?" Alexandra provoked, losing patience.

"No, I don't. Women use me... for my mind... for my body," he stated playfully, the comment earning him another open-mouthed gawk.

Alexandra finally giggled, the sound going straight to his groin.

"Cool, maybe he'll hit on me and ask me out," she said with a mischievous leer. Roman gave her one of his patented scowls. "What? Even my parents reminded me last week that I'm twenty-three almost twenty-four... I'm chronically single... never had a boyfriend... and according to them, they are getting older, and they want a grandchild before they are too old to enjoy it—"

With that, she went silent and refused to make eye contact.

"I know things didn't go well with that asshole Scott Turner," Roman consoled, hating to see her in this condition. "I wish you had told me you two *weren't* dating."

"What did you say?" One of Alexandra's perfectly shaped brows rose.

Roman stiffened.

"Scott Turner only went out with you because he wanted you to do a feature story on him for the *'NYC's Up-and-Comers'* column." He glanced away as he mentioned, "Also what kind of man makes a woman pay her own cab fare after a date?"

"I never told you about my date with Scott Turner, and I definitely didn't tell you I had to pay my own cab fare home," she grilled, suspicion masked her features.

Not wanting a lecture, he tried diminishing his comment by redirecting the attention away from himself.

"I knew that guy would be an asshole," he practically growled. "He's got shifty eyes and he sweats a lot."

"Definitely," she agreed, knowing that Roman was using his redirection strategy on her, something he had done since high school. "I don't think I'll ever meet a decent guy, especially in the crazy media industry."

"True, but in his defense, dinner at The Dutch was a brilliant move as far as sucking up goes. I've been trying to get reservations to that restaurant for over a month."

"How did you know he took me to dinner at The Dutch?"

"I just know." He refused to elaborate. "Plus, Scott Turner is not your type anyway."

"How would you know that?" she glared.

"You've told me, several times in fact." Brow wrinkled before he asked, "Why won't you tell me what your type is?"

"It's none of your business, that's why," Alexandra replied with an angry huff.

"I'm your best friend," Roman declared. "I should have known that you were single."

"Are you serious?" She rolled her eyes at him knowing it drove him crazy, choosing to avoid his latter statement. "I didn't tell you, *'Mr. I'm-God's-Gift'*, because not everyone is a magnet for the opposite sex."

"I'm no magnet," he insisted. "If you haven't noticed, I've been on a drought lately. I haven't had a date in forever."

"Don't make me laugh, Giordano. If you think a year without a girlfriend is a drought, I should join a convent right now," she educated, feeling even worse about her own love life or lack thereof. "Try a lifetime desert with no rain clouds in sight. Ever. When that happens then we can compare notes."

"I can't argue with that," he grinned. "Now can we please get back to work?"

# VIII

It wasn't surprising that after Roman left the morning seemed to go a lot smoother. Without the gorgeous editor-in-chief looming over her desk, asking questions she had no idea how to answer while staring at her like he was a death row inmate and she was his last meal, everything fell into place. If she didn't know better, she'd think he was actually interested in her more than a friend.

At noon, she met with her first source, Mark Macintosh, co-owner, and head of public relations at Macintosh & MacGyver, who gave her all of the information she needed to write a great story on the new sports arena near the Hudson River. And to her surprise, the man did *accidentally* brush his palm over her butt. An even bigger surprise, he *did* ask her out. She even considered it for a brief moment, and then let him down easy. After all, she didn't want to burn a bridge she may need to cross in the future.

Her second meeting went well too. Kyle Mendez, her source at the public works department, kept his hands to himself and also gave her solid leads on where to track down the missing funds at his company. The only thing that didn't make sense to her was he asked her out as well. Two men, who were both cute and single, gave her a second look and a third look and a fourth.

*Yup! Today she was definitely a man-magnet.*

Her self-esteem soared as she finished her extremely productive day, and before she knew it, it was time to call it quits. At five thirty she began packing her briefcase to go home to her small, yet adorable studio apartment in Soho. All she had left was figuring out what to buy for dinner: Indian or Greek. A gyro sounded good, but so did mild Butter Chicken with basmati rice and garlic naan. Unfortunately, she wasn't a good cook, even though she came from a long line of incredible Southern cooks. It was common knowledge that every time she made toast her smoke detectors went off.

"Alexandra, don't pack-up yet." Roman's deep voice startled her out of her own head. "Just got a call from, Sylvia. She wants a mock write up of the public works story with sample photographs and she wants them before midnight."

"Does that mean—"

"Yup!" he interrupted. "Overtime, overtime, overtime."

"No way!" Alexandra responded, dropping her briefcase back on her desk and plopping onto the seat like a bratty kid. "I've been here since eight this morning. I was just thinking about what to have for dinner and which episode of *'Forever Knight'* to watch.

"Did you know this was going to happen too?"

"Unfortunately, I did."

"This really sucks," she moaned. "I just want the day to be over. Do we really have to work overtime?"

"Stop complaining, rookie," Roman playfully scolded. "I can order some take-out. What would you like?"

"What about gyros?" she grinned. "I'm in the mood for Greek food."

He contemplated her suggestion before saying, "Sure, gyros coming up."

"You are a damn good boss," she genuinely complimented.

"Is that so?" he snickered, blushing.

"How long is this gonna take, I mean to get the article ready?"

Truthfully, Alexandra didn't mind working overtime. The extra would be used to pay down her credit cards, but being around Roman today was getting stranger and stranger. Several times she caught him staring at her cleavage or checking out her butt. It was so unlike him, and it was wigging her out.

"Several hours," he replied, concentrating on keeping his gaze on her face. "Less if we don't get distracted."

"Will this day ever end?" She grimaced.

Roman gave her a mock pout.

"May I make a suggestion?" Roman interjected. "We'll work from my place. I'll even cook dinner."

Her eyes lit up at the offer. Roman was an amazing cook. Always had been. In high school he would make her homemade pizza, calzone, pastas of all types, plus any dessert that she requested. Chocolate was usually an ingredient.

"Only, if you make your famous Spaghetti ala Carbonara with your special garlic bread."

"Deal!" he grinned. "Now pack up and let's get out of here. The rain is coming down in buckets.

He had done it! They were no longer going to the café, and that small change might be the factor in ending the deadly loop. All he could do was pray that it worked.

C'mon, soldier, move it," he teased, pretending to be a drill sergeant.

"Did I sign-up to be a news reporter or a marine?"

"There's no difference." He winked as he graced her with a huge, lop-sided, boy-next-door grin exposing the dimple on his right cheek. Thankfully, he didn't see her swoon. As usual, her heart did that old pitter-patter thing whenever he was around. She was such a goner.

"Fine, I'll go."

"Like you have a choice," he smirked.

"Then spaghetti at your house is perfect," she beamed.

"We can eat while we work."

"There's that word again; *Work*," she sighed and pretended to pout. "This better be some fantastic dinner, Roman."

As they rode the elevator down to the lobby in comfortable silence, Alexandra hummed along to the muzak playing on the overhead speakers. *You Give Love a Bad Name* started, but only she started doing an air guitar accompaniment in the elevator, not caring if the night watchman saw her on the security camera.

"What's the matter?" She stopped in mid-strum. "We always play air guitar to Bon Jovi."

# Four Past Midnight

"I'm just sick of this song that's all. And I'm sick of playing air guitar. I think I might start listening to opera," he stated matter-of-factly, the stunned expression on his friend's face made him smile.

"Whatever you say, boss." She leaned against the smooth metallic wall of the elevator. "Do you think the rain will let up anytime soon? We could wait a few minutes."

The elevator doors opened when they gently touched down on the main lobby floor.

"No, the rain's not going to stop," he answered with finality. "We should leave now."

Before she could protest, he moved her quickly, leading her by the elbow toward the front doors.

"Why are you walking so fast?" she complained breathlessly. "I've got shorter legs than you and I don't appreciate having to jog alongside of you like Bruno."

"I'm sorry, but I wanna get home before it really starts to pour," he informed, anxiety fueling his strides.

"Whatever you say, Roman." She shivered as the cold air hit her jacketless form.

Roman remained pensive, unable to relax until they were safely at his place. He couldn't relive another night that ended in Alexandra's death. It would surely drive him mad.

"I wish I had brought my raincoat," she mumbled.

Those words loomed over him like a shroud and this time he began to shiver, but not from the chilly weather.

Taking off his trench coat, he draped it around her slender shoulders, directing her as she put her arms into the sleeves, which were much too long on her. Without asking, he folded the extra material until it was the perfect length.

"I love it when you pretend to be a gentleman," she teased, looking up into those seductive emerald, green eyes.

"I'm always a gentleman." He made a face.

Then he opened the lobby door, and stepped out first, opened the large black umbrella, and covered her as she followed. Avoiding the fat raindrops, they huddled under the device, their bodies rubbing together in that delicious way. Alexandra smelled wonderful, as always, with her expensive *Chanel* perfume. It was the only guilty pleasure she allowed herself.

"Hold on a second." She tugged on his elbow making him come to a complete stop. "I want to buy a muffin from the café."

"Now?" Eyes narrowed to hard slits. "I'll get you another muffin tomorrow morning with your coffee."

"I can't wait that long," she stubbornly argued, shaking her head. "I want to eat it while I watch television tonight."

She batted her long, dark lashes, knowing he could never resist when she did.

Of course, he reluctantly gave in.

"Alright, but we have to hurry," he insisted with an exasperated expression. "I don't want to be working on this project after midnight."

## Four Past Midnight

Quickening their pace, they walked to the corner café where she bought a chocolate chip muffin for later, and then they both made their way back to the front entrance. The streets were still bustling with people, natives and tourists alike. All of them moved with a single purpose, to arrive safely at their final destinations. People of all races, colors, and creeds huddled together, sharing umbrellas. It was an amazing sight to see.

"Change in plan." He tugged her sleeve bringing her to a halt. "I'm not in the mood to walk in this weather. Let's take the subway."

"Why?"

"That intersection is really dangerous." His shoulders shrugged automatically.

So, they turned around and made their way in the opposite direction, totally bypassing the dreaded corner and the crosswalk.

"You can't be too safe crossing the street in the big city," he reminded the Florida native, the growing pit in his stomach deepening. "Especially in downtown Manhattan where the cabbies are notoriously fast drivers."

"Whatever you say, boss."

"What time is it?" Roman asked, the rain assaulting the synthetic, black material of his umbrella.

Alexandra pushed the sleeve of the expensive *London Fog* trench coat up a tad to glance at the face of the gold wristwatch she wore.

"It's only five forty-five," she answered, readjusting her sleeve once again. She heard him let out a long, slow breath. "Are you in a hurry to get home to Bruno?"

She giggled as they walked to the subway entrance only a few feet away from the café.

"Ha! Ha!" Roman threw his dark locks back in a mocking laugh, suddenly righting himself and giving her one of his patented *'if-you-weren't-my-best-friend-I'd-kick-your-ass'* glares, which only made her giggle more. "What can I say, Bruno is more interesting than a lot of people I know."

"Is that so?" she scoffed.

"That's right," he snickered, nudging her hip with his briefcase. "Especially some women I associate with,"

"Touché," his friend replied, hanging her head low in mock shame.

Roman grinned as the gears in her mind started to turn.

"But what does that tell you about the women you associate with, not me of course," she clarified, "the *others*."

A streak of jealousy made her look away.

"That's a low blow," he responded with a grimace.

"It's not my fault the four-legged ball of fur is able to keep your attention when so many women failed to do so," she insulted, holding up her hands in a sign of surrender.

*She was definitely jealous.*

"I'll let that slide since I have someone to go home to, and all you have is… *wait*… never mind," he teased. The well delivered jibe hitting her like a punch to the gut.

"Great comeback, you are so much better at insults than Bobby Lieberman. Did I ever tell you he tracked me down on *Facebook*?" she snorted.

The news made him stop abruptly.

"No, I think I'd remember you telling me your childhood nemesis was stalking you on social media."

"Last month he sent me a friend request," she awkwardly responded. "Can you believe it?"

He shook his head in surprise.

"Me either."

"What did he want?" The suspense was killing him.

"He… he wanted to apologize." She smiled innocently.

"Are you kidding?"

"Nope," Alexandra sang, using his all too familiar sing-song manner. "He explained he had anger management issues because of family stuff, and he basically begged for my forgiveness."

"Wow!"

"Then he told me he had a crush on me in high school," she snickered.

Roman stopped again, a sudden violent surge filling his body at the thought of Bobby Lieberman wanting to date his Alexandra.

*That's right. His.*

"He asked if I'm planning to visit my folks this Christmas."

"Why?"

The anger in his voice must have been evident because she shot him a surprised look before continuing.

"He wants to take me out to dinner," she shrugged, wiping a few raindrops that had landed on her face.

"You said, no… right?"

"Of course, I said no," she glared, surprised he would have to ask.

"Good." Relief replaced his anger.

"He's a guidance counselor at our old high school," Alexandra chuckled. "Isn't that funny?"

"Yes, yes it is." An amused snort escaped him.

Out of the blue Alexandra added, "I'm debating if I should get a pet."

"Absolutely not!" Roman rebuked, shaking his slightly, overly long, jet black locks.

Immediately, she glared at him.

"No more goldfish! No more canaries! No more animals of any sort," he ordered, contorting his face. "You are forever banned from ever owning another pet."

She started to defend herself, but he continued.

"And don't argue because the topic is closed."

"You're not the boss of me—"

# Four Past Midnight

He interrupted again.

"Pretend I am. And technically, I am the boss of you." Roman gave her a stern stare. "Trust me it's better this way."

"I can't believe you're trying to tell me what to do," Alexandra protested his over exaggeration.

"Do you want another animal tragedy on your head?"

"No," she mumbled under her breath.

"If you want to you can come over and play with Bruno whenever you like," he mocked with a snort earning him an eye roll.

"In my defense, I'm positive Mr. Fuzzy had an eating disorder. And he really did show signs of bulimia."

He paused to glare at her.

"You've got a mental disorder from eating all of those chocolate chip muffins."

"Don't be mean," she grumbled. "I'm older now, wiser."

There was only silence as he studied her.

She thought he was finished when he suddenly added, "I'll make you a deal. If you can survive being in the same room with a lizard, I'll support your decision to buy another pet."

Her eyes widened in horror, and he knew he had her exactly where he wanted her.

"That lizard attacked me!" She contorted her hands in an attack position and made a weird hissing sound.

"I know, I know, a deadly attack lizard," he scoffed, making her feel like a complete moron. "She bit your finger and you panicked. I remember. You called me grief-stricken when she escaped through your bedroom window."

"It's not surprising that it attacked me. Did I ever tell you once I had a dream that Izzy morphed into a Velociraptor and chased me through the Everglades?"

Roman couldn't contain his laughter any longer. Her humor always made him feel better.

"You're right though," she finally admitted. "A pet wouldn't be a good idea, now that I've reexamined my past track record."

A sigh escaped her.

"Thanks for reminding me of my pet failures, Roman." Her tone dripped with sarcasm, which she didn't bother hiding.

"No problem." Emerald, green eyes sparkled playfully under the New York City streetlamps. "Happy to oblige."

# IX

At a few minutes past six they were entering the lobby of Roman's apartment building, known to the rest of the city as *The Valeria*. The impressive edifice named after Roman's great grandmother was a classic 1950s-style white-brick structure located between Union Square West and Fifth Avenue on 14$^{th}$ Street. It had been built in the early 1960's and contained approximately two hundred units divided between two wings and over ten floors.

"Good evening, Mister Giordano." George, the doorman, greeted them as he held open the glass door that led into the main lobby. "Miss Martin."

"Hello, George," they both replied in unison.

The lobby always made her stop and stare. A lofty ceiling decorated with a Venetian mural similar to *The Pope's Ceiling* at the *Sistine Chapel* in Vatican City mesmerized everyone who walked through. Three grand, golden chandeliers hung majestically overhead while smooth gray and white streaked Venetian marble stretched seamlessly across the floors. Hand-painted murals of the Venice canals, gondoliers, and intricately placed stone fountains adorned the walls adding to the building's old-world sophistication.

"This place always takes my breath away." Alexandra's awed expression was mimicked in her voice.

Her girl-next-door beauty made his member harden.

*Damn it!*

"Me too," he agreed as they glanced around at his family's pride and joy. Discreetly he used his briefcase to hide his misbehaving cock.

Roman had mentioned once that the apartment sizes in the building ranged from studios to three-bedroom units. *The Valeria* had its own full-time staff, 24-hour attended lobby with doorman and a live-in superintendent. The building also featured laundry rooms on every floor, exercise facility with a personal trainer, even an on-site valet service and its own parking garage accessible from within the building.

Located a half-block from Union Square, *The Valeria* was steps from all major subway lines which made it a perfect location in itself. Not to mention, a well-known farmer's market they frequented on weekends was only a few blocks away. The impressive indoor market specialized in local organic produce, fresh seafood, high-quality meats, and other specialty items too numerous to mention. It was only a short walk to neighboring areas which included the Flatiron District, Gramercy, Chelsea, the Village and the Meatpacking District.

It was perfect, like its owner.

"It's really coming down out there, isn't it? Good thing you're sharing an umbrella," George the doorman observed with a broad smile and a playful wink.

"Sure is!" they both spoke in unison.

# Four Past Midnight

"I haven't seen you around much, Miss Martin." The bright-eyed, sixty-something year old stated with concern as he followed a few feet behind as they made their way across the lobby toward the elevators.

"I know," Alexandra grinned. "My boss is a real workaholic. He's trying to send me to an early grave."

She giggled at Roman's pointed stare as they continued walking.

George laughed, but he didn't mind.

"I know the feeling," the doorman added. "My boss is a real ball buster as well."

All three laughed then.

"We've got work to do, rookie," Roman tried to move them along without insulting the doorman who he considered to be a friend as well.

He had known George for as long as he could remember. When Roman was a kid, he'd hang out with the kind man after school until his parents or grandparents got home from the family businesses. George would always take time to play card games with him or help him with his arithmetic homework. Yes! George was as good a friend as Alexandra.

Roman steered her into the elevator, turning and placing her body in front of his so she wouldn't see the bulge in his pants beneath his suit jacket.

"You two are hilarious," he jibed sarcastically, maneuvering her with a firm hand placed at the small of her back right above her ass, purposely letting his hand linger a little longer than it should have.

"Are you trying to cop a feel, Mr. Giordano?" his friend inquired with a chuckle.

"Possibly, would you mind if I did?" his voice lowering to that sexy whisper she'd always loved.

"Very funny, I'm not your type," she reminded with a disapproving glare.

"There you go with that *type* thing again." He shook his head.

"In all the years I've known you, you've only dated tall, long-legged, voluptuous supermodels." Her lovely doe-eyes narrowed.

"Really?" he gulped, realizing she was correct. "I hadn't noticed, but since you keep pointing it out, I guess it must be true."

"Of course, it's true. I'm a reporter. I'm paid to notice details," she taunted.

"If you're so detail oriented, Miss Martin… tell me… how many of these *'types'* of women have I dated?"

She watched him quizzically.

"In high school, during college, or more recently?" Alexandra challenged.

"Start from high school and end with my relationship a year ago," Roman smirked, leaning against the smooth mahogany wall of the elevator. "Go ahead. Impress me."

Without hesitation she listed: "Anna-Beth, Rhonda, Cybil, and Diane in high school. While you were attending Columbia you dated Jessica, Tamara, and Liz. Then more recently there has been Martika, Elaine, Margret, Candy—"

"I got it." He blushed at the number of women he had gone through in such a short period of time. "I'm a slut."

"Yes, you are," she announced, irritation hanging off her statement.

George cleared his throat, trying to ease some of the growing tension.

"Are you two burning the midnight oil again?" the astute man observed. "You're young, you need to relax a little, have some fun."

"I agree," she chimed in.

Although she had never been very good at having fun. Unfortunately, she relied on Roman to force her to have fun. Without him, her life would be as boring as drying paint.

"Keep it up," Roman said, hitting the button for the elevator doors to close and take him out of the line of fire. "Don't forget, I'm the one who signs everyone's paychecks."

"When are you two gonna settle down?" George stepped into the verbal mix. "You know, the missus and I got married right out of high school. It was the best damn thing I've ever done. Forty-five years of wonderful."

"Umm," Roman sounded flustered.

*Why weren't the damn elevator doors closing?*

"We're just friends." Alexandra answered for them both, her cheeks suddenly became heated.

"Best friends," he clarified, still trying unsuccessfully to get the elevator doors to shut.

"I married my best friend," the man continued. "Have I showed you a picture of my new granddaughter? One month old next week."

"We really have to go, George," Roman informed as the doors *finally* began to close. "I'll talk to you later."

"Have a good evening," the enthusiastic doorman requested, tipping his hat as the doors shut.

"I've always liked him," she mumbled to herself.

"Yeah, he's quite a character." Roman massaged his nape.

"Can you imagine being married to someone for forty-five years?" she exhaled in awe. "Incredible."

The elevator dinged, informing them they had reached the top floor. Quickly, Roman entered his access code and the doors slid open to let them out right outside of his apartment door.

"After you."

Patiently, he waited for her to disembark then followed, unlocked his front door, and guided her inside to the foyer, where he helped her out of his trench coat and rested his keys on the console table. They were met by Bruno, carrying a half-eaten rawhide bone, and looking overjoyed by their presence.

"Hey, boy!" she keened with enthusiasm, patting the dog's head, and then scratched his exposed belly when he turned over onto his back.

"Traitor," Roman chuckled at his dog's ability to ignore the person who fed him.

"You're not a traitor," Alexandra replied to the adorable pooch.

"I'll be right back," he said, grabbing Bruno's leash, the umbrella and a small plastic bag. "I'm gonna take him out before the rain gets any worse."

"I'll come with you—"

"No!" he practically shouted. "Stay here where it's—" he wanted to say safe, but settled for, "—dry."

"If you insist," her melodious voice wreaking havoc on his senses.

Roman and Bruno left her alone, returning almost fifteen minutes later. The extremely expensive designer suit he wore was soaked and he was shivering. His teeth chattered to the point that the sound resembled a jackhammer.

"What happened?" she gasped, taking the leash out of his hand and releasing Bruno from the clasp.

The dog shook the excess water off of his fur and ran into the living room to lie in front of the radiator.

Roman dropped the umbrella on the foyer floor before he explained.

"A gust of wind blew the umbrella out of my hand. I'll be fine. Bruno, on the other hand, may never go out in the rain again. It's coming down in buckets."

Slowly and with great effort, he took off his jacket; his dress shirt was drenched as well.

"Get out of these wet clothes before you catch a cold," she said, her maternal instincts kicking in.

"Yes, ma'am." His hands shook as he tried to unfasten the buttons of his sopping dress shirt. "I can't feel my toes."

"Good gracious," she huffed. "Here, let me help you."

Yanking his trembling hands away, she made quick work of unbuttoning the garment and tugging it off, letting it land on the floor beside her. Roman's skin felt like ice.

"I don't want to have to take you to the hospital if you catch pneumonia," she commented, trying to ignore the fact that he was still shivering. "Stand by the radiator you'll warm-up faster."

Taking his freezing hands in her much warmer ones, she began to rub them briskly.

"How's that?"

The heat from the radiator felt good against her body so she knew it felt even better to him considering he was a human popsicle.

"Much better." Roman struggled with the clasp and zipper of his trousers.

"I've got it," she reassured, concerned he really would get sick. His entire body was shivering now, even though the heat from the device was at full blast.

"Sunshine," he began to protest, but she was already unbuttoning the clasp and lowering the zipper, heartfelt concern distracting her from her rather inappropriate actions.

# Four Past Midnight

When she grabbed the waistband and began to pull the clinging material down his legs, Roman's body stiffened. Ignoring him for the moment, she fought with the article of clothing, determined to free him from the frigid confines. For several moments, she worked the trousers down his toned legs, stopping briefly to remove his drenched socks and shoes, before finally maneuvering the pants completely off.

With a satisfied grin she exclaimed, "All done."

However, when she looked up into her best friend's shocked face. A gasp tore from her throat as she noticed during her exertions, she'd knelt in front of him and was now staring at his barely confined member. The fabric of his black, cotton boxer briefs tented to its limits.

*Holy moly!*

In all of her imaginings, she'd never imagined... *this*.

"O-oh, my g-god!" she stammered, unable to unglue her eyes from his crotch. She had seen a couple of dirty movies on the *Playboy Channel*, but she was certain she'd never seen any porn star with a cock quite so massive. The sheer size of it mesmerized her, causing her curiosity to overshadow her embarrassment.

"Alexandra—"

"Do you stuff it with rolled-up socks or something?" her voice lowered, fascinated by the fact the humongous appendage seemed to be growing right before her bulging eyes. Curiously, she made a motion to touch it, when she felt Roman's strong grip on her wrist, his annoyed glare warning her to stop.

A small grin suddenly played on his lips as he said, "Sunshine, if you touch it—" his deep voice raspy like he'd just stumbled out of bed, "—be prepared to use it."

Realization slammed into her, and heat flooded her cheeks as she quickly stood, knowing with him it wasn't a threat. He would make her follow up with *whatever* he deemed appropriate.

She was a virgin in the fullest sense. She had never... ever... sucked a man's cock. She'd touched one once, in college on a dare. But that one was nothing in comparison to Roman's super-sized—

"Alexandra," his deep chuckle brought her out of her thoughts. "Get your mind out of the gutter."

"If I had my rain jacket you would have been dry as a bone," she lectured, blushing again.

"I'd rather catch pneumonia than wear that ugly thing," he admitted with a smirk.

On cue, she stuck out her tongue.

"Would you like something to drink?" Roman graciously offered, needing to clear his lustful thoughts.

"Water, please." Her smile returned.

"Coming up," he stated bowing low then turned and walked to the kitchen with almost all of his delicious body out in the open and on display.

*Dear father!*

Was he really going to walk around like that, half-naked and in that condition?

## Four Past Midnight

Suddenly, she felt hot. Not hot like the heat was on too high. *Hot like wanting to rip those boxer briefs off and see what all the fuss was about concerning big—*

"You look flushed," Roman commented from the kitchen. "Is it too hot for you?"

Embarrassment filled her completely, chasing away her naughty ideas.

"No... you're fine."

*Damn it! Did she say that out loud?*

"I mean... it's fine in here... not too hot."

His eyes narrowed, but he didn't remark any more about her state of agitation.

Trying to hide her embarrassment, she looked around admiring his home. The place was gorgeous. An open floor plan with cathedral ceilings and lots of natural light, adorned with marble and natural stone accents, hand carved moldings and baseboards that were original to the building that probably cost a small fortune themselves. However, even with all of its expensive furnishings, it was still tasteful and unpretentious, just like Roman.

"Did you redecorate?" Alexandra questioned, giving the room a thorough once over. "It looks different."

"A little bit," he admitted shyly.

He hated talking about his money.

"My grandfather's taste was on the old-fashioned side," he educated. "Mine is more contemporary. So, I incorporated a little of both."

The fully restored three-bedroom two-bath unit was immaculate. After all, Roman was almost as OCD as she was when it came to certain things. He took great pride in being neat and organized. His father drilled that into him from the first day he worked in the kitchen as a dishwasher. His dad said it made sense for him to learn the business from the ground up like he did. So, when Roman was old enough to reach the countertops in the family-owned restaurants, his father put him promptly to work as a dishwasher/busboy, then waiter, finally, line cook.

Her gaze drifted to the new custom-made window treatments.

"Did you decorate the space yourself?"

"I had a professional decorator do it," Roman beamed, admiring how well it turned out. "I told her what I liked, and this is what she came up with."

Her hands touched the arm of the imported Italian leather sofa.

"I like the neutral color scheme: the whites, creams, beige, and the way she did the furniture placement."

Alexandra knew being a guy he didn't care about how things coordinated or clashed in a space, let alone if it achieved a consistent flow from room to room. He just cared if there was a gigantic flat screen to watch sports and movies on.

In the living room, his furnishings were elaborate consisting of an antique armoire, full-sized, cream leather sectional sofa and two matching armchairs paired with a hand-carved mahogany and glass coffee table he had commissioned with a local artist, after discovering the man's work at an art festival in Soho a couple years back.

Not being much of a shopper, he kept most of his grandfather's belongings and left it up to his mother who visited him at least twice a year to buy things she believed to be necessary. His one indulgence item was an enormous eighty-inch, flat screen television, which he named *Mona*. According to him, it was not only his right as a *guy* to purchase the television, but his obligation… whatever that meant. After all, she didn't speak '*guy*'.

To her right, a wall of floor-to-ceiling glass palladium windows ran along the entire back wall of the living room, overlooking Central Park. French doors leading out to the open air, wraparound balcony offered an incredible view of Manhattan at night, all twinkling lights above and swaying treetops below. Yes! She could live here. After a tough day of chasing stories for the newspaper, she could imagine relaxing on one of Roman's outdoor lounge chairs while cool autumn breezes caressed her skin and wake the next morning to a cup of coffee enjoying a view of a fiery New York sunrise of bronze, crimson, and cobalt. It was awe-inspiring to say the least.

"If it wasn't raining, we could eat on the balcony."

"Next time," he promised, an unknown expression blanketing his face.

She turned to face her friend and saw that he was staring at her. Not an innocent look between two people who had known each other for many years, but something *more*. Suddenly, she felt uncomfortable.

Clearing her throat, she asked, "Are these the original floors?"

"Say that again," he requested, moving closer, their shoulders touching. Their proximity making her think very inappropriate thoughts like how those shoulders would look naked and glistening with baby oil. She'd seen Roman shirtless many times, and each of those times she thought she'd faint from his beauty. Now here he was, standing beside her, wearing only boxer briefs and a smile. The reality was she wanted to see him completely naked.

*What was she thinking? It was definitely inappropriate to want to see your best friend of almost a decade naked. She was such a pervert.*

"Are the floors original to the apartment?" she repeated through the frog currently residing in her throat.

"Unfortunately, no," he frowned. "The original oak flooring had to be removed. This new hardwood was expensive, but it was totally worth it."

"Here you go." He handed her a glass of ice water.

"Thanks," she said, avoiding eye contact so he wouldn't see her guilty expression. "I see you had the kitchen remodeled too."

He shrugged those muscular shoulders.

"I figured it only made sense, ya know, might as well do all of the renovations at once and get it over with."

Needing to put some distance between them, she walked over to the breakfast bar and ran her palm over the smooth surface.

"Is this granite?"

"No, it's quartz," he switched back to innocent banter. "I liked the pattern. It's unique."

"It is," she nervously agreed.

Sensing her growing apprehension Roman continued their small talk.

"My mom helped pick out the cabinets. She claims they're not too masculine and they're easy to maintain."

"Your mom definitely has good taste," Alexandra agreed with a grin.

The kitchen was all polished cherry cabinets, dual stainless-steel sinks, and all new stainless-steel appliances. He even splurged on a walk-in pantry allowing him to stock-up on all of those imported Italian ingredients his mother would send him. And a newly built laundry room housed state-of-the-art washer and dryer units.

She wasn't surprised the walls had no color.

"Khaki walls?"

"Yeah," he answered, rubbing the back of his neck. "You know me. I like earth tones, nothing too bright, no lime green or orange or turquoise."

"I know. Your idea of wild and crazy is sage green," she jokingly teased.

She couldn't help the chuckle that bubbled to the surface. He stuck his tongue out and she wanted to suck it into her own mouth.

*Hell! What was wrong with her tonight?*

Without warning, he was standing beside her again, his voice lowering to that seductive timbre once more.

"So," he added, slipping an arm around her waist. "Tell me what you really think."

He knew she'd always be honest with him, no matter what.

Clearing her throat and taking a deep cleansing breath, she thought of dead kittens to get her libido in check then responded with: "I think the apartment is the perfect representation of you: comfortable, subtle, and elegant. I love everything about you… *it*… I mean *it*."

Her foot lodged in her mouth, and she wanted to excuse herself and go jump off the balcony. Thankfully, the only reaction Roman gave was a small smirk that appeared on his expertly crafted, full lips.

"I'm glad you love *it*."

"Has your dad seen it yet?" she queried, taking a small sip of her water to keep her voice from cracking.

"Not yet," he replied with irritation.

Leonardo, Roman's father, wasn't thrilled when his only son told him he didn't want to become a head chef or CEO for the family's chain of Italian restaurants. Instead, he wanted to be a journalist. Let's just say the shit hit the fan and was still raining down. Louisa, his mother, didn't care. She only wanted their son to be happy, but his dad practically threatened to disown him if he didn't run the family business.

Stubbornly, he refused to accept his dad's threats, worked his way through college, relying on part-time jobs and scholarships to finance his education. Thank goodness she had helped him bring his grades up in high school. Otherwise, he might be working at his father's restaurant chain feeling trapped and miserable.

# Four Past Midnight

It was truly a miracle that all of Roman's financial troubles disappeared when his grandfather passed away a year ago and he inherited a small fortune in stocks, bonds, and annuities, in addition to *The Valeria*. The entire building belonged to him. The penthouse apartment was where his grandparents lived before they retired to Florida, while he and his parents occupied one of the larger three-bedroom units on the floor beneath.

It was ironic that he paid nothing for his Manhattan penthouse while she paid a small fortune for a cramped studio in Soho. Once he had offered, actually it was several times, to let her live in one of the vacant units in the building for free or rent for significantly less than what she was paying now. Awkwardly, she refused, telling him she didn't feel comfortable with either of those propositions. She never wanted him to feel she was taking advantage of his generosity. He often told her she was insane. Sometimes she agreed.

"Make yourself comfortable," he urged as he headed toward his bedroom. "I'll be right back. If you need to freshen up, you know where the guest bathroom is."

"Uh huh," she responded, trying to admire the gigantic space instead of Roman's firm buttocks as he walked down the hallway.

Searching for a distraction, she put her umbrella in the holder in the foyer, took off her shoes, and played with Bruno until he returned. Unfortunately, none of that helped. Naughty images of Roman pinning her to the newly installed quartz countertops flickered through her over-active mind.

"Bruno must really love you." Roman's voice startled her.

The man did wonders for a pair of loose-fitting black sweatpants that hung deliciously off of his tapered hips and a body-hugging white tank.

"He doesn't let anyone else, besides me, give him belly rubs. The last time my mom visited he almost bit her finger off."

"At least someone in this apartment has excellent taste," she mumbled.

"What was that?" Roman called from the kitchen.

"Nothing." She blushed.

"Missed me?" he asked with a wink.

"Yes, you promised to feed me, and you haven't yet," she told as her stomach made a loud growling sound. "I'm getting ready to faint from hunger."

"How about some antipasti?" her friend suggested, and she nodded her agreement.

Gracefully he walked to the refrigerator, opened the door and peered inside. The spacious unit was neatly packed with anything and everything you could possibly need to prepare a mouthwatering meal.

"I have Cotto salami, Kalamata olives, some imported Mortadella…"

"Surprise me."

She always felt overwhelmed knowing she was so far beneath him on the social ladder. Her idea of antipasti was cheese and crackers.

# Four Past Midnight

"I have a bottle of *Tesoro della Regina Pinot Grigio* in the wine fridge," he proudly announced.

"No, thanks." She grimaced.

"Are you sure?" he asked, gathering the ingredients together along with a large, wooden chopping block and an intimidating professional chef's knife.

"You know I'm a light weight," Alexandra reminded. "I might get a little tipsy and start doing a striptease or something equally embarrassing."

Both brows hitched below his hairline before he said, "Now, that I'd like to see, you do a striptease. I could turn on some music."

The challenge in his eyes was unmistakable.

Nervous butterflies began dive-bombing inside of her stomach.

"Never in a million years," his friend chuckled.

"Too bad," he teased, a sexy pout drawing attention to his regal mouth. "I've always wondered what you look like underneath those clothes."

"Stop that," she mumbled as heat engulfed her entire face.

"Stop what?" He smirked, knowing his comment made her uncomfortable, but truth be told he really would love to see what she looked like naked.

That was all it took for his cock to instantly spring to life.

*Damn!*

"Alexandra, haven't you ever done anything wild and crazy before?"

Narrowing her eyes she swore, "No, I don't like wild and crazy. You of all people should know that. I prefer safe and boring."

"Too bad," he mumbled below his breath. "I'd like to do wild and crazy things to you."

"What was that?" She honestly didn't hear what he had mumbled. "I didn't quite hear you."

"It was nothing important." His semi-hard cock disagreed with his statement.

"Do you need a hand?" she questioned, wanting to be helpful.

He looked at her. The innocently spoken words made his member grow another painful inch.

"Pardon me?"

"Do you need a hand getting dinner ready?" Alexandra repeated.

Blowing out a breath he didn't know he was holding, he reassured her by saying, "No, thanks. I can handle dinner. You should get started on the article. I already know exactly how we're gonna arrange it."

"Great!" she cheered. "It shouldn't take very long then."

"If we don't take any breaks, we'll be finished in three hours tops," Roman encouraged.

"Sounds good to me." She stood and looked around the space. "Is your laptop in the study?"

# Four Past Midnight

He nodded yes.

"I'll get it."

Roman watched her perfect ass swaying as she sauntered down the hallway to his home office. The ripe, round body part unknowingly mocked him, and he couldn't hold back the groan that escaped his chest. A few minutes later, Alexandra returned carrying his laptop. Sitting at the dining table, she began.

"Okay, boss. How should I start the article?"

# X

Soon they had a groove down. Roman relayed his ideas to her as he made the food while she arranged and wrote his suggestions, expanding on them to complete the write up.

Thirty minutes later, he proudly announced, "Dinner's ready!"

Now starving, he rested both bowls of steaming Spaghetti Carbonara on the breakfast bar along with a full basket of garlic bread, a bottle of wine for him and a soda for her.

"Let's eat before it gets cold."

Quietly, they sat down, immediately digging into their dinners.

"I forgot what a great cook you are," she flattered, twirling a healthy portion of pasta onto her fork.

"I should be after four years of working on the line at my father's restaurants," he stated confidently, opening the bottle of pinot.

"Mmm," she hummed, the sound going straight to his groin causing him to shift in his seat. Discreetly, he adjusted the linen napkin on his lap trying to hide the evidence of his arousal.

"I take it you like it?"

# Four Past Midnight

He watched her with appreciation. Alexandra always had a good appetite. She wasn't like most of the women he knew who ate a salad and claimed they were full.

She swallowed.

"I love it!" She beamed her appreciation. "You have to teach me how to cook."

"Absolutely not," he declined, shaking his head.

"Why? I'm a quick study."

"Yeah, you're a quick study at journalism, not at domestic stuff," Roman critiqued.

"I resent that," his best friend huffed, eyes narrowing.

Gathering a fork-full of pasta in one hand and holding a piece of garlic bread in the other, Roman informed, "It's the truth."

Shocked at his flippant tone, Alexandra glanced up from her meal.

"Remember when I made my mom's chili?" she recalled. "That turned out well."

Roman's right eyebrow arched.

"I remember having diarrhea after eating it."

Rolling her eyes, she promptly corrected him.

"I told you; my chili didn't make you sick. It must have been something else you ate."

"If you say so." He snickered.

They sat for almost half an hour, chatting and joking over the day's events and past mistakes. Roman laughed until he thought he would cry when Alexandra told him how she had to bribe one of her contacts in college by flashing her boobs.

"I love the story of you showing that guy in college your tits!" he exclaimed, wiping away a tear at the corner of his eye.

"What was I supposed to do?" she pouted. "Lose my best lead. Dean Smith's affair with the women's basketball coach, Mrs. Reynolds, was front page news. Plus, I never liked that woman. Something about her eyes. They were shifty and she always smelled of mothballs."

Roman laughed. The sound ran along her spinal column and settled in her sex.

"You are hilarious!" he complimented as he enjoyed their comfortable conversation. "And before you ask, yes, I'm a guy and if I had the opportunity to see your breasts I'd jump at the chance."

"Too much information," she blushed at the thought.

Inadvertently, he glanced at her cleavage then quickly refocused on her eyes.

"I didn't mean to over share," he grinned.

"Oh!" she exclaimed, looking back down to her empty bowl. "Thank you for dinner. As usual, it was delicious."

"You're welcome." He graced her with a boyish grin.

"It gets too cold here and I hate the snow," she added absent-mindedly then took a small sip of her soda. "I miss the year-round warmth of Florida. Don't you?"

"I hated those muggy summer nights," he openly admitted.

"I thought you loved it there," she gasped, taken aback by his admittance.

"The only thing I ever liked about Florida was you." He immediately glanced at her trying to gauge her reaction.

"What did you say?" Alexandra asked shyly.

"It's true," he explained and nodded his head for emphasis. "I can't imagine life without you."

"I didn't know you felt that way," she purred, giving him an appreciative look.

"I've shared that with you," he said leaning closer, the faint scent of his cologne making her lose her ability to think clearly.

Alexandra began shifting uneasily in her seat.

"You were so happy-go-lucky in high school," she told, wanting him to know how she saw him. "I thought nothing fazed you."

"Nope." He moved a little closer, an emerald gaze fixed on her and she was afraid to look away. "If you hadn't stumbled into my life who knows where I'd be."

Her uneasiness faded as she stared into those deep, emerald pools.

"I think that's the sweetest thing you've ever said to me." She blushed.

"Really?" Feeling vulnerable, Roman shrugged off her comment and quickly changed the subject. "I'd dreamt of attending Columbia University since I was ten when my elementary school took a field trip to the campus. I loved those impressive buildings and well-kept commons."

He paused before continuing.

"I've told you this story before."

She shook her head no.

"I thought I had."

He knew he had, but he'd keep that bit of information to himself. No need for her to think he truly was one egg short of a dozen.

"I've never seen you nostalgic," she revealed, feeling more drawn to him than before. "It's nice."

Then suddenly a glazed look came over his rugged features as he announced, "Yeah, remembering all of those half-naked babes, makes me long for the good old days."

His eyes sparkled playfully, and she knew he was only joking.

"You are such a pig!" She threw the napkin at his head, hitting him between the eyes.

"Seriously, though," he continued, taking her slender hands in his, enjoying the way they fit together. "You are the most important person in my life and I'm grateful to be able to call you my best friend, and I wouldn't have met you if my parents hadn't moved. Those four years we were apart during college were miserable."

"You never mentioned that before," she beamed. "I thought you were living out a dream."

"Don't get me wrong," he added. "I had fun, but not having you in the same city was difficult."

"You're sweet. I missed you too," she wholeheartedly admitted.

"Why did you have to go to FSU anyway? Why Tallahassee? You had your pick of great colleges: Yale, Princeton, and Berkley," he inquired, rubbing his thumbs over her quickening pulse.

*Good gracious!* If he didn't stop now, she'd spontaneously combust.

Shrugging her shoulders she stated flatly, "It's a family tradition. Both my parents went there and so did their parents."

"I wished you would have followed me to New York. We could have been bad together." He waggled his eyebrows suggestively, making her blush.

"You are acting so weird today. It's freaking me out... *a lot.*"

She looked down at their intertwined fingers and then gently pried them apart.

"By the way, you were right," she announced, looking at him once again, a large grin on her face.

"What was I right about?"

Roman took another serving of pasta, offered her some more, but she declined.

When she hesitated, he took a bite of the room temperature food.

"Macintosh."

Swallowing the mouthful of pasta in a large gulp, he asked, "What about Macintosh?"

"The jerk grabbed my butt," she huffed, rolling her expressive brown eyes.

"I told you." He sang like a four-year-old. "But I can't say that I blame the guy. After all, you do have a fine ass, Miss Martin."

Alexandra suddenly choked on saliva that went down the wrong way when she gasped at his inappropriate comment.

"Damn it!" he exclaimed, patting her on the back. "Are you okay?"

"No, no, I'm not," she sputtered, trying to regain the ability to speak. When she was finally able, she continued. "And he asked me out. So did the other guy. Surprised the hell out of me."

He paused, fork hovering almost to his mouth.

"Are you gonna go out with one of them?" The jealousy he felt surprised him.

"I'm not sure, probably not." She smiled at the thought though.

"Good," he stated, relief filling him.

Alexandra took a long drink of her cola.

"What was your reason for not accepting their offers?" he questioned, hoping she wouldn't realize how much the idea of her dating someone else bothered him.

"I don't want to ruin my professional relationship with them, in case I need information in the future," her explanation was reasonable. Alexandra always did have a good head on her shoulders.

"Smart thinking, rookie," he complimented, letting out a sigh of relief.

After dinner, it only took them three hours to finish the article. Roman faxed the write-up and within ten minutes the owner gave him the thumbs-up to print the story. It would be in tomorrow morning's early edition on the front page, 'Breaking News,' but he still couldn't help the worried expression painted on his face.

"I guess I'd better get going."

Alexandra stood, stretching her arms above her head, the movement calling attention to her perky breasts. Roman adjusted his growing erection as discreetly as he could.

"What are you going to do now?" She glanced around the spacious living room at the television set.

He stood as well. Their height disparity allowed him to see down the vee of her dress to the plump mounds hiding beneath.

"I'll probably watch some type of sports," he revealed, shrugging his shoulders while he admired her long tresses.

For some reason, he'd always been in awe of how shiny and curly it was. Perfect inky spirals, except in high humidity weather like tonight. Tonight, however, her hair hung in perfect straight layers over her shoulders to the middle of her back. It took all his willpower not to reach out and touch the shiny tresses.

"What about you?" he asked, but he already knew the answer.

"I'm going to watch reruns of my favorite show," she answered in that off-handed way that she had.

"I don't know how you can watch the same thing every night." He laughed. "Aren't you sick of that show?"

"No!" she gasped. "I'll love Nick always."

"You're insane," he smirked, walking her to the door, instinctively checking out her ass.

Alexandra had a drool-worthy butt. Tonight, he wanted to grab it. He remembered how perfectly the firm globes fit in his palms the night before.

"Who wouldn't enjoy a drama about an eight-hundred-year-old vampire working as a police detective in modern-day Toronto."

"And why would he do that?" Roman indulged her, wanting to hear the rest of it.

"Isn't it obvious?" the woman smirked. "He becomes a cop in order to atone for centuries of killing innocent people, and in the process of helping others he hopes to find a way to become human again."

"Interesting," he concluded, not wanting to admit it sounded like a unique spin.

## Four Past Midnight

"I know, right," she smiled then and he forgot about everything else except her. "It's getting late. I should get going."

"It's already late," he relayed, trying to conceal his guilty thoughts, and not ready for her to go home yet.

"I know," she said with a frown. "But I'm tired."

"We can watch Forever Knight together. Here," he suggested, desperate to have her stay a little longer. He was positive she would be safe if they didn't leave the apartment until after four past midnight.

"How are we going to watch it?" she frowned. "It's not scheduled to play on cable tonight. I was going to watch it on my DVD player."

"The last time you were here, you programmed it to automatically record the episodes, remember?"

"I forget about that," she admitted with a wide grin. "You didn't erase them?"

The last time Roman made dinner for her, she took the liberty of programming several of her favorite television shows into his DVR and as well as adding them to his streaming channels. She figured that he would never *'accidentally'* forget to pay his bills, so they would be available to her to watch if she *'unintentionally'* forgot to pay hers.

That was logical.

"No, I kinda forgot about them," Roman confessed, observing her yearningly.

"You're pulling my leg." The woman planted her hands on those lush hips.

"Humor me." He continued, trying to hide his horniness. "I wanna see what all the fuss is about with this series."

"You're serious. You want to look at Nick with me?" she scowled. "This isn't one of your stupid jokes?"

He shook his head no.

"Please," he begged. "I'm dying to see what all of the fuss is about."

His choice of the word dying didn't sit well with him, but regardless, to his delight, she gave in.

"Fine, but you can't make any negative comments during the show," she demanded.

"I promise," he said giving her a genuine, toothy smile.

After a second or two, Alexandra nodded, her dark tresses caressing the sides of her face.

"I guess it's alright. After all, you did make us a very lovely dinner."

He grinned, knowing she wasn't going anywhere and for the moment she would be safe.

*Thank you, Detective Nicholas Knight!*

An hour later Roman smiled and shook his head.

"That wasn't half bad." The admission made him want to pull out his own tongue.

"Did you really like it?" Alexandra's broad grin showed two perfect rows of white teeth.

"I'm ashamed to admit it, but yes, yes I did."

"I knew you would. See, I'm not crazy." She gave him a playful slap.

"Well, I wouldn't go that far," he teased mischievously.

He dodged a decorative pillow that whizzed past his head.

"Careful!" he exclaimed, grabbing both of her wrists when she went to throw another one.

"You're so mean to me," she condemned with a giggle, maneuvering her body so she could kick him, almost landing one in his private area.

"Watch your feet!" He used his much larger and heavier body to pin her to the sofa. "I'll need that one day."

"Who would want to carry your little monster offspring?" her words were choppy due to their erratic movements.

"You'd be surprised," he said, tickling her sides, enjoying the sounds of her squeals. "I'm quite a catch I've been told."

"In your dreams, Roman," she panted. "Stop it!"

With all of her might, she pushed against his chest, but the man was a solid wall of muscle.

"Admit I'm a catch." He continued his assault.

"Yes, you're a catch!" her squeals became deafening. "I'm sure some aboriginal tribes in the Amazon would find you perfect."

"Why are you so stubborn?"

The feel of her wiggling under him caused his cock to harden again, but this time instead of trying to hide his arousal, he rubbed against her hip. Immediately, she stilled like she had been hit by a freeze ray. Before she could protest, he bent, brushing his lips to hers. The softness of her full lips pulled a low growl from his chest. After a few seconds he pulled away. He looked down into brown eyes wide with shock and his heart began to pound within its confines.

"What are you doing?" she asked, touching her lips with her fingertips.

"I'm kissing you." He swallowed hard, lips burning to be against hers again. "I'll stop if you want me to, but I don't want to."

A long pregnant moment passed as she pondered his words. His body still pinned her against the soft leather sofa. Instinctively, one of her hands rested against his chest holding him at bay while the other still pressed to her mouth.

When he thought she'd push him away, she surprised him once again by reaching up, entwining her arms around his neck and pulling him down to her. The feather-light touch of her lips made him shiver. Wanting her to continue, he let her take the lead as she devoured his mouth with gentle nips, luxurious glides and sensuous licks. His arms began to shake.

With all of the strength he could muster, he gathered her up in his arms and stood. He wanted her so badly he could barely think, barely complete a sentence. All he could manage to say was, "Bedroom... *now*."

Alexandra held on tight as Roman carried her to his room, their lips still pressed firmly together.

"Roman?" she mumbled against his mouth.

"Huh?"

"I think you've forgotten something... something very... important." She felt herself being lowered onto the bed.

Suddenly he stood, stripped off his tank top and shoved his sweatpants down his muscular legs, leaving only his black boxer briefs on. She couldn't contain the gasp that escaped her chest as he stood staring down at her like a man who had lost all of his self-control.

He resembled a statue she once saw in a history textbook of the Roman god Jupiter. High regal cheekbones, straight nose, soft, sensuous full mouth, black inky locks hanging loosely over one emerald eye in that all too sexy gaze, and muscles rippling and flexing every time he took a breath. She allowed her eyes to wander further down his torso, over his well-defined eight pack, down his lean, tapered hips, to the trail of black hair that led from his bellybutton down to his—

"My God!" she gulped when her eyes made contact with the enormous bulge currently trying to break free of his underwear. He was the epitome of sex! Glorious and wild and passion-filled and he wanted her.

A soft chuckle brought her back to the scene currently playing out before her.

"You're gonna make me blush if you keep eyeing my goodies that way."

"Roman." She swallowed what remaining moisture she could muster before adding, "I've never had sex, remember?"

That did it, the corners of his mouth turned down transforming his face into a mask she couldn't read.

"Have you ever had a… *virgin*… before?" She hoped he hadn't.

For a long moment he stood there, looking at her from different angles, then left, disappearing into the ensuite bathroom. A few seconds later he returned holding a soft, thick bath towel and a few foil packets.

She gulped again.

*Shit! This was really happening.*

"We don't need those," she confessed, nodding at the condoms.

His forehead crinkled with confusion.

"I'm on the pill."

His expression still looked puzzled before she clarified saying, "I have terrible cramps during my period. The doctor prescribed them to help manage the pain."

A look of relief suddenly washed over him, and he took a deep cleansing breath.

"That's good to know," he replied with a smile. "I've never done this with someone like you before, but I promise to be as gentle as I possibly can, okay?"

She nodded her consent.

"Do you think it's gonna hurt?"

The worried expression on his face was the only answer she got.

*Great!*

Holding out his hand, he helped her stand.

"I need you naked, Sunshine."

Suddenly, he reached down and grabbed the hem of her dress then slowly inched it over her thighs, hips, mid-drift, torso, chest, finally yanking it up and over her head. He dropped the garment at the foot of the bed. Nervously, she made a move to cover her chest, but he halted her with a gentle tug on her arm.

"Please, don't hide from me."

His gaze drifted over her in a heated caress, until it landed on her heaving breasts.

"Take your bra off," he ordered with an air of command that made her legs tremble.

Acting on pure adrenaline, she did as she was told, a wave of nervousness washing over her.

"Fucking beautiful," he expressed with a sigh which made her blush.

Impatiently, he reached out and ran the back of his hand over her right breast then turned his hand, so his palm came to cup the heavy mound. His lightly calloused thumb made small circles over her tightly beaded nipple. Closing her eyes, she tried to keep herself from fainting. She'd never let anyone touch her like this before and she wondered why. It felt so naughty.

Without hesitation, he leaned down and blew over the peak making it harden to the point of pain, but before she could protest, he lowered his head and took the point into his hot, wet mouth. Mischievously his tongue drew invisible circles over it until she thought she'd scream from the pleasure of it.

"Mmm," he growled, the vibrations sending need from the point where he teased her, down to her womb, finally pooling in her now soaking sex.

She squeezed her thighs together to keep the ache from increasing.

"You taste so good, Sunshine. So good."

With a wet pop, he released the aching bud and found its twin, lavishing the other nipple with just as much vigor as the first. Her legs really did buckle then, but Roman encircled her waist and held her securely in place with two strong hands. The subtle scent of his cologne filled her mind with more lustful thoughts.

"Are you alright?" he asked when her breathing had stopped.

The only response was a nod of her head.

"Alexandra, if you hold your breath, you're gonna faint, and then I'll have to take you while you're unconscious." He chuckled.

Her lips parted to curse at his comment, but he sealed his mouth over hers before she could call him whatever terrible thing that had come to mind.

# Four Past Midnight

This time he was in complete control doing wicked things to her. He licked and nipped and explored every part of the area leaving nothing to the imagination at the things he could do to her with that talented pink muscle of his. When she thought she couldn't take anymore, his tongue sought hers out and sucked the tip into his mouth. The constant pulling action made her clit begin to pulse to an almost painful beat.

It was both heaven and hell.

"Roman, please." She heard the words but didn't recognize who said them. The raspy sound of her own voice sounded foreign to her ears.

"Enjoy it." His gruffly spoken words ignited her desire as he took her hand and guided it to the waistband of his boxer briefs. "I want you to touch me."

Filled with nervous knots, she waited, not sure exactly what he wanted her to do. Sensing her unease, he took her hand and slipped it inside the waistband and placed it directly on top of his rock-hard member.

Alexandra touched him… *there*. Her hands stilled as he began to rub his cock against her slightly sweaty palm. He didn't seem to mind as he allowed her to touch what she guessed was his shaft.

*Holy hell!*

*She was jerking off her best friend!*

"Up and down… not too hard, yeah, just like that," Roman practically whimpered.

The feel of steel encased in silk was a sensation that sent her mind into overdrive. Guttural moans of pleasure spurred her on to move lower until she held his heavy balls in her hand.

"Lightly run your fingernails over them. Damn! That feels amazing."

Moving to the side of her neck, he adjusted his head to get a better angle. Starting below her left ear, he began a slow trail of wet kisses that made their way south across her graceful neck down to her collarbone. She jumped when he gently nipped her skin, and then swiped his tongue over the area to soothe the sting.

Instantly, he stopped, concern filling his voice as he asked, "Did I hurt you?"

"No, you surprised me," her whispered answer seemed loud in the stillness of the bedroom, and their heavy breathing echoed throughout the large, well-decorated space.

Moving lower, he kissed a trail down the valley between her breasts, continuing further over the sensitive skin of her torso, abdomen, and finally... *finally*... he dropped to his knees and landed directly over her fabric-covered mound.

"Wait," she pleaded, looking down at him with a nervous expression. "I've never liked the idea of someone doing... *that*... to me. It's so *unsanitary*."

He laughed, stopping abruptly when her expression changed to an annoyed glare.

"Let me have a little taste. If you don't like how it feels, I'll stop."

# Four Past Midnight

Contemplating his words for a couple of seconds she unenthusiastically nodded her consent.

Then he reached up, and hooked his thumbs into the black lacey material of her panties and slowly drew them down her slender legs. Alexandra wasn't a tall woman, 5'4" to be exact, but she had long, lovely legs for someone her height. He stopped for a moment to run his palms over the silky skin admiring the smoothness of them.

"Step out," he ordered when the strip of fabric pooled at her ankles.

Obediently, she did.

"Widen your legs for me... *perfect*."

He used his thumbs to spread her lower lips, the evidence of her arousal glistening on her puffy folds.

"You're so pink."

At his observation, Alexandra's body suddenly stiffened.

"What's the matter?"

"Nobody's ever seen me naked before," she explained, her expression glum. "I know I'm no supermodel. My tummy is a little soft. I think it's from those muffins I like so much, and I know I should probably exercise... and my breasts... just look at them."

"I am looking at them, can't take my eyes off of them and I think every inch of you is gorgeous. I just want to eat you up."

She began to say something when he interrupted.

"Just. Like. This." He punctuated each word with a flick of his tongue to the swollen bud at the apex of her thighs.

Again, her body stiffened at the unfamiliar sensation he was creating.

"Roman," she hissed through clenched teeth, holding onto his muscular shoulders to keep upright.

Ignoring her, he held her thighs with a firm grip knowing that the moment his mouth made contact she would try to slam them together.

"Don't fight it, *relax*."

Her body softened a little.

"There you go," he praised. "Look at me."

The words didn't quite register until his mouth came down once again, latching on to her lower lips.

"Holy shit!" she whimpered, her legs almost giving out.

Skillfully, he adjusted his shoulders, using them as a wedge between her widely spread legs as he began a slow exploration of her sex.

"You taste sweet like candy," he announced as his tongue slid leisurely along her labia, halting its progression to nibble on her lower lips.

His declaration made another rush of arousal seep from her core.

"I can't wait to be inside of you," he whispered.

Spearing his talented muscle, he began to plunge inside her slick entrance, and then without warning, he breached her opening with one thick digit.

"Oh!" was the only word that came to mind through the haze of desire surrounding her brain.

Rapidly, Roman worked her clenching depths with knowledgeable movements, stopping occasionally to lightly nip and roll her clit between his lips.

"Alexandra," he keened, beginning to suck her swollen bud with more gusto. "Think about how good it's going to feel when it's my cock inside of you instead of my finger."

Truthfully, the thought terrified her.

"Roman," she mimicked his sound, grabbing a handful of his hair. "I think… I'm… *coming!*"

The tensing of muscles inside her channel almost broke his fingers. Ripples of passion shimmied from her sex to her abdomen then outward until every limb shivered from the bliss it created. If this was how an orgasm felt, sign her up for another one!

"*Wow!*" she exclaimed in a loud, throaty whisper. "Now, I know what all of the fuss is about."

A large grin spread across her illuminated face like a light had been turned on beneath her skin.

"You can do that to me anytime."

Suddenly, Roman stood. His face tense with need… the need to have her. Every fucking inch of her.

"I'm not done yet," he informed as he began to push down his boxer briefs. "There's more."

His rough tone creating another set of ripples, but this time they were heading down to her sex.

"I'm nervous," she admitted without shame as he helped her sit on the edge of the mattress.

"Me too." His lips set in a thin, hard line.

Touching his cheek with a gentle stroke, she asked, "Why are you nervous?"

"If I'm terrible, you'll always remember it because I was your first."

Gently, he pushed her backwards until she was lying flat on her back.

"Go towards the middle of the bed."

She felt the bed dip as he climbed onto the massive king-sized bed with its padded leather headboard and taupe and white bed linen. It looked like something you'd find at the *Waldorf Astoria Hotel*.

"That's true," she teased, earning her an amused grunt.

When he was within touching distance, he adjusted her legs until they were spread as wide as he could get them, bending them at the knees, and making her lift her lower body to place the towel beneath her hips.

"If I'm really good," he grinned and arched one brow. "Then I'll forever be remembered as the man who all other men have to live up to."

# Four Past Midnight

Roman hesitated. The thought, for some reason, of another man touching her didn't sit well with him, but he brushed it away with a shake of his head.

Alexandra giggled; the sound made his cock flex like it was being controlled by some horny puppet master.

"You'll be named… Roman… Italian god of sex."

"Damn straight," he chuckled. Boldly running his palms over the sensitive skin of her inner thigh, and then settled his body between her spread legs, their groins rubbing provocatively against each other.

*Jeez! He hoped she wouldn't be so tense.*

"Stop holding your breath and just relax, Sunshine," he chuckled. "It's no fun if you're unconscious."

Glaring at him, she huffed, "That's easy for you to say. You're not the one getting ready to be impaled by a blunt projectile."

Taking a deep, steadying breath, she then released it in a slow, steady stream.

"Okay," she exhaled, squeezing her eyes shut like she was bracing for a shot or something equally unpleasant. "Just do it."

"This isn't a shoe commercial," he chuckled, smoothing back the black tresses that were clinging to her flushed cheeks. "I want it to be incredible for you. Do you trust me?"

She nodded without hesitation causing his chest to do that strange tightening thing it had been doing all day whenever they were in the same room.

"Kiss me," she ordered with a slight smile. "Now, before I change my mind."

He didn't have to be told twice. Bending slightly, he took her face between his hands, placing soft kisses at the sides of her mouth.

"Your lips are so soft, Alexandra." His palms relished the supple skin beneath them. "Why haven't we done this sooner?"

"Because you're an idiot," she stated bluntly, wiggling her body against him.

Unexpectedly, Roman moved to her neck, drawing slow, maddening circles on her over-heated skin with the tip of his tongue. "For once I have to agree with you."

"Stop talking and take me."

She wiggled her naked form trying to get his attention, soft breasts smashed against his much harder chest. Their combined body heat made him perspire, but he didn't care. Before she could speak again, he claimed her kiss-swollen mouth.

Finally, she pulled away and managed to whimper, "I need you."

Releasing her lips, he admonished saying, "Be patient."

When she stilled, he made his way down her body, bypassing all of the other tasty parts of her form until he ended at the entrance of where he was dying to be. Slowly, his fingers parted her folds and without hesitation he sunk one long, thick, finger into her hot, wet depths.

"Holy cow!" she moaned.

# Four Past Midnight

"Damn, you're so tight," he hissed, unable to think clearly as her flesh hugged his digit.

"Roman," she whimpered. Her entire body was going rigid as the unfamiliar object registered in her lust-hazed brain. Before she could complain, he began to ease it out, not quite removing it completely, then with pain-staking slowness pushed it back inside of her entrance all the way to the second knuckle.

"Breathe, Sunshine… breathe," he ordered again, the scent of hot, aroused woman filling his nostrils and pushing him closer to the animal need to claim her hard.

After a few seconds, her body relaxed and her legs widened for him, as her hips began a slow circular motion against his hand.

"Don't stop," she begged, on a low husky growl.

Leaning forward, he gave her swollen bud several long, sinewy, swipes with his tongue. Alexandra's sweetness hiking up his arousal another notch as his cock grew another inch.

*Fuck!* His balls were in so much pain he thought he'd die from it.

Withdrawing his finger completely, she pushed up onto her elbows and gave him a sullen pout making him chuckle. With just as much care, he added a second finger into her channel, amazed at the tight fit. He wondered if he'd be able to fit all of himself inside the extremely tight confines of her body.

*Fuck yeah! He'd make it fit.*

If he died from the pleasure of being inside her then so be it.

Finally, he added a third finger, sliding in and out of her a little easier due to the trickle of cream weeping from her core.

"Are you ready?" he asked, hoping the answer was a resounding *'yes.'*

A nod of her head and the heated gaze she graced him with were the only answer he needed.

Without further ado, he knelt between her spread legs, lined his cockhead to her sopping entrance, holding it firmly at the base, and then swiped it through her folds coating it with as much cream as he could gather. This was easy since she was so turned on. Gradually, he began to push inside, stopping when he was only a couple of inches in.

Both of their eyes widened as the tip of his cock hit her maidenhead. Before her panic could take voice, he pushed through. A pained yelp accosted his ears as her body turned to marble and her knees locked his hips in place. Tears began escaping down her flushed cheeks as she held her breath.

Thinking of a way to distract her, he questioned, "Did you know I've wanted to jump your bones since high school?"

She shook her head.

"Well, it's true."

He pulled his hips back allowing his cock to slide out about an inch then pushed slowly back inside.

"I remember I had stayed after school for tutoring, and you were late for our meeting. Do you remember?"

"No," she huffed on a whisper, her nails digging into the tops of his shoulders.

# Four Past Midnight

"You were coming from soccer practice, and you were wearing the cutest little navy shorts with the white piping at the hem. Your legs looked tanned and sexy. I thought you were *hot*."

"Why didn't you ever tell me that before?" Alexandra squeaked, holding her breath.

"I didn't want you to feel uncomfortable with me," he said, kissing the tip of her nose.

"Roman—" Her sentence came to an abrupt end as he pushed past her tightly gripping inner muscles.

"Jeez!" he proclaimed loudly, the tight fit even tighter than he imagined.

"Damn!" Alexandra moaned and tried to close her legs, her motion stopping him from entering any further. Needing her to be calm, he bent, claimed her lips and demanded entrance. A second later she opened for him, and his tongue didn't miss a beat.

Instantly, he found her pink muscle, lavishing it with wet lashes and long sucks on the tip he hoped would drive her into a sexual frenzy. He was right. Thank goodness! Her legs relaxed once again, and he pushed in a little further until almost half of his hard-as-nails member was seated.

"Hell!" was all he could say.

"You're too big," she chastised against his lips as her lower body lifted off the bed in a spasm.

"Should I stop?" Roman gritted his teeth.

*Please don't say 'yes'.*

When she didn't say anything else he tried to push in another inch, both of their eyes widened again. Reaching between their bodies, he located the tiny bud between her legs peeking out of its hood. Coating his finger in her cream, he started to draw invisible circles on her clit with the tip of his middle finger. He breathed a sigh of relief when another trickle of her arousal coated his shaft. Instinctively, he pulled out again, only an inch or so and then pushed in another couple inches, continuing the circular motion with his finger.

"Mmm," she purred arching her back off of the mattress. Her more than ample breasts tempting him to have a taste, so he did.

Abandoning her full, pouty lips he bent lower, surrounding her beaded cotton-candy, pink nipple with his mouth. Using his tongue, he teased and licked the delicious nub with the tip. When she arched more, he closed his lips around it and began a steady sucking motion causing it to harden even further.

"Shit!" he moaned against her overheated flesh, the vibration making her squirm with need. Releasing the peak he went for its twin, licking and suckling until she began to meet him thrust for agonizing thrust.

Quickening his pace, he fought his way inside her heat and sighed when he was finally... *finally*... fully seated... balls deep. The sudden realization hit him hard. Here he was, buried inside of paradise where no man had ever been before. Smiling, he suddenly heard the theme to *Star Trek* playing inside his head. *Captain Kirk* would be so fucking jealous.

"Don't stop!" she hissed again, her voice bringing him back to reality.

He began to really move then, withdrawing and advancing, finding that wonderful pace that made her moan and him curse. Being inside of the tight space was both pleasure and pain, agony and ecstasy, her body gripped him like an unyielding vise giving him no quarter. And her moans, her moans were the most erotic sounds he'd ever heard, soft cries of passion and deep growls of lust. She was his every fantasy come true.

"Look at me, Sunshine," he commanded, wanting, no needing to see her when she came. Needing her to know that he was the one to take her to the edge of reason. "I want you to remember this moment, always."

She smiled as she pulled his mouth back down to hers. Boldly, she slipped past his defenses as she sucked the tip of his tongue just as he had done to her, applying a steady suction that he imagined her doing to his cock. That was all it took.

"I can't holdback anymore, Alexandra!"

The tightening of his balls warned of his eminent release.

"I need you to come," he announced, as his hips began a wild pounding into her clenching depths.

"Oh… my… God!" she yelled, body tensing, back leaving the mattress almost bucking him off. At the same instant, hot jets of molten seed shot into her hungrily clenching core, the sensation of tiny fingers forcing all of his liquid arousal into her. Collapsing on top of her, he quickly shifted his body to the side so he could press against her still heaving breasts without crushing her.

"Holy shit!" Words finally came to him. Not the eloquent ones he hoped for, but the only ones he could currently form.

Panting breaths slowed to a more reasonable pace before she whispered, "I never... *ever*... thought it would be so—"

"Fucking perfect," he finished her sentence.

She giggled as her fingers ran through his hair, massaging his scalp.

"I can't believe we just did that."

The reddening of her cheeks was one of the most beautiful things he'd ever seen. He couldn't resist the urge to kiss her shoulder blade, the closest body part to his mouth, so he did.

"We should definitely do that again," Roman encouraged, giving her a playful nudge with his elbow. "Are you sore?"

"A little," she sighed. "But in a good way."

"Yeah." He wrapped one arm around her waist and hugged her tightly. "That should break the damn circle."

Suddenly, she sat up, pulling the covers over her naked form.

"What circle?"

"That déjà vu thing that's been going on. There's no way in hell fate could see that plot twist."

He chuckled and made the mistake of looking directly at her and was met by a look of betrayal marring her beautiful face.

"What's the matter? Why are you looking at me like that?"

"You made love to me to break this idiotic time loop fantasy you've got going on?"

# Four Past Midnight

Her brown eyes began to fill up with unshed tears.

"You planned this." Her hands waved frantically between them.

"No, I wanted to have sex with you," he freely admitted.

Actually, his re-hardening cock wanted a repeat performance right now.

"And I sure as hell didn't want one of those *other* guys to hit it before me."

*Fuck! Why did he say that?*

"Excuse me?" Alexandra's eyes widened, nostrils flared, and her mouth did that pursing-thing that told him to cover his man parts. Sitting up he grabbed a nearby pillow and rested the down-filled barrier over his member.

"Shit!" He wiped his hand over his face with frustration.

Shouldn't they be spooning right about now or maybe starting another round of foreplay? Having a knockdown, drag out fight didn't seem like the right post-coital ritual.

"That didn't come out the way I meant it."

"Then clarify, Roman. Right the hell now."

"For the last several days, all I have done is lose you. Every damn day something happens to you and then it starts all over again. I'm going crazy because I can't seem to fix it… fix this," he confessed, waving his hand wildly between them. "I can't keep losing you. I can't do it anymore." He covered his eyes like a small child.

A strange expression appeared on her tense face right before she whispered, "You're insane."

"I'm not insane. Not yet anyway," he chuckled like a crazy person, cementing her observation.

"So, you wanted to make love to me?" She watched his reaction closely.

"Of course, I did. Why would I want you to die a virgin… again?"

His head snapped up, emerald eyes to brown, he couldn't mistake the hurt he saw in the deep, chocolate depths.

"So, this," she pushed him away. "Was a pity fuck?"

He paused, only upsetting her further.

*Damn! Damn! Damn!*

Like a fleeing leopard, leapt off the bed, tears freely falling now as she swiped at them with angry motions causing his heart to tighten, and he had to rub his chest to ease the ache.

"You're overreacting, Sunshine."

*"Don't call me that!"* she shrieked, her eyes bloodshot and puffy. *"Don't you ever call me that again!"*

He sat up, exposing his manhood, hoping to lure her back to bed.

"What are you doing?"

"I'm going home," she answered between sniffles, the sound of her in pain causing him to feel like the dog that he was. Even Bruno, who had pushed the door open and lay at the foot of the bed, snarled at him then grabbed his rawhide bone in his mouth and left for a safer spot to loiter.

"Please." He stood not caring if he were naked or not. "Come back to bed. Let me explain."

"Leave me alone," Alexandra snarled.

As he reached for her elbow, she stepped backwards almost tripping over her clothes, and before he could clarify, she was already slipping on her panties and reaching for her black bra. His mind went blank as he stood stock-still watching her dress. The sight of her breasts bouncing with every motion made his cock swelled more.

"I want you to stay."

"Why?" She stopped momentarily to glare at him.

"Why... what?"

"Why should I stay?!" she snapped, slender hands placed on her nipped-in waist, hair mussed in that sexy *'I've-just-had-my-world-rocked'* sort of way, looking much to sex-goddess-like to leave now.

The minute it took for him to answer seemed much longer. For the life of him, he couldn't come up with a reason except, "Well, I hoped we could do *that* again."

*There went his foot again.*

"Ugg!" Like a whip she swung around, her long, black hair streaming behind her fleeing form like a shiny cape blowing in her wake.

"I'm sorry. It's not as bad as it sounds." He tried to reason, tried to make her see his intentions were indeed honorable that he wasn't just trying to tap-that-ass, but change their destiny as well. "I'm an idiot. We both know that. I can admit it. Damn it! Alexandra, for God's sake—"

"Get away from me, Roman!"

In two strides, she reached the bedroom door, turned the knob, and yanked it open. He swore the hinges pulled away from the frame.

"At least let me take you home."

He looked down for his sweatpants but didn't see them. He was completely naked and ready to follow her downstairs.

"Please slow down! I need my pants!"

"No," she whispered. "You've done enough, thank you."

By this time, she was fully dressed and was heading toward the living room where she found her shoes and briefcase. With a puppy dog look of regret on his face, he followed.

"Sunsh—" She shot him a look of death, so he quickly amended. "Alexandra?"

"Please, leave me alone!"

Her sobs attacked his nervous system, and the sight of her crying too much for him to bear.

"Honestly, I don't understand why you are so upset. We just had the most incredible sex... wild, mind-numbing, blow-your-socks-off sex. You should be on cloud nine."

Halting in midstride, she turned to face him, tears falling once again.

"I love you, Roman."

The declaration battered his ears like a drummer's wails on his skins. He stood motionless. Afraid to move. Afraid to blink.

"Did you hear me?" She sniffled. "I said, *I love you.*"

"I heard you," he whispered like they were in a confessional, and he was a priest.

"Well?"

"Well, what?"

Her glare intensified as she inquired, "Would you like to say anything to me?"

"About what?"

He wasn't trying to be dense. He really was dense.

"*Ugg!*"

She ran out of the apartment, into the hallway and pressed the button for the elevator, rage replacing her tears.

"I quit!" She spat the words out like a viper spits venom.

"You can't be serious."

*Where the hell did he put his pants?*

"You bet your ass I am," she confirmed, tapping her foot impatiently. Anxiously, she pressed the button again, mentally willing it to arrive faster.

"You can't quit your job."

Then realization hit him. He was now standing in his birthday suit for all of the security guards monitoring the hidden cameras to see. *Perfect!*

"You're under contract. I could sue you for the violation of… of…" His treacherous mind went blank.

"Fine, then sue me," the woman snarled, daring him to continue. "I don't give a rat's ass! You can kiss my ass for all I care. It's all the same to me."

"If you come back inside, I could definitely kiss your ass," he joked, trying to lighten the mood, but the furious female wouldn't listen.

"Goodbye, Roman," she stated flatly as the bell sounded letting them know the elevator had finally arrived.

Quickly, she stepped into the space, pushed the lobby button, and stared at her shoes, and then Alexandra Martin said the worse thing anyone could say to another person. "I hope you have a good life."

And with those words hanging over his head like the blade of a guillotine, she was gone.

After a shocked second, the reality of the situation hit him hard. He was going to lose her if he didn't confess his feelings for her. Quickly, he sprinted back into the apartment, past a very irritated Bruno, down the hallway, to his bedroom, where his sweatpants were hiding under the bed mocking him. As fast as he could, he donned the pants, and then found his tank over by the closet door.

*Shoes… shoes… where the hell were his shoes?*

# Four Past Midnight

*Ah ha!* They were also hiding under the bed, probably in cahoots with his pants.

He glanced at the alarm clock at the side of his bed and cursed a blue streak. It was four past midnight.

"Fucking woman… had to leave… sonofabitch… not again… please damn it… not again," he rambled, trying to get his feet to move faster. Thank goodness he remembered to grab his trench coat before he left.

Like a man possessed, he sprinted back to the elevator, pushed the button, and impatiently waited.

"Fuck this shit!"

He ran to the emergency stairwell and flew down over ten flights of stairs until he made it to the empty lobby. Up ahead, a crowd had gathered outside near the front of the building.

"Fuck it all to hell!"

About to lose his dinner, Roman pushed past all of the people, the crowd thick with onlookers, all wide-mouthed and grumbling frantically. A familiar face came into focus. It was George.

"Mr. Giordano!" The doorman was sobbing and clutching his cell phone, his knuckles white from the force.

"What the—"

"She was crossing the road—" the older man tried to explain.

"Not again," Roman felt his stomach drop. "Alexandra?"

Taking another step, he looked down, and felt the life drain out of him and onto the pavement where she lay with her eyes half open staring at him.

"I already called an ambulance," George sniffled, wiping his nose with the back of his uniform sleeve. "I got the guy's license plate number, the asshole. The police are looking for him."

"Roman," the woman he loved gurgled as he fell to his knees beside her. "I'm sorry—"

"Shh," he begged, smoothing back that crazy hair of hers, the rain transforming it to its regular spiral curls.

"I don't wanna—"

"It's gonna be okay," he lied, feeling the pit of his stomach begin to lurch again. "Help is on the way, Sunshine. I'm sorry, Alexandra or maybe Miss Martin?"

She gave a weak smile. Grabbing his hand in hers, she confessed, "I really do love you… even if you don't love… me… back…"

And with that said, her eyes closed.

"Alexandra?" He smoothed her forehead with his thumb, her face growing cold from the raindrops beading there. "Open your baby browns, Sunshine. *Damn it! Open your eyes!*"

Then he took her hand in his and felt her wrist for a pulse. It was there, but it was weak.

"Please, look at me."

The gasp of the crowd and the peal of the ambulance sirens were his only response.

# Four Past Midnight

"Is s-she... gone, Mr. Giordano?" George was sobbing again.

"Not yet!" He screamed, the tears starting all over again. "Alexandra, don't you leave me! Do you hear me? Don't you fucking leave me! Not like this!"

"Mr. Giordano." George knelt beside him; his eyes redder than his own. "The ambulance is here. It's here."

Violent trembles had taken hold of his body as he screamed.

*"Alexandra!"* He was hugging her tightly, cradling her limp body in his arms like he would a sleeping baby.

With determination, the paramedics pushed through the growing crowd, but by that time they had to practically pry him off of her.

"Sir." The male EMT touched his shoulder, but he ignored him. "We've gotta get her to the hospital. You need to let go. Please, just let go so we can take care of her."

Still, he didn't listen. He knew even if they went to the hospital, it would all end up the same with Alexandra dead.

"Open your damn eyes," he ordered, his tone harsh and furious. "C'mon... open your eyes... open your eyes and talk to me."

"Sir, we have to go," the EMT said in a more forceful tone.

"Alexandra, it's me the slave driver, the womanizer."

"Sir!" the man barked. "We have to get her to the hospital. You can meet us there."

"I'm her cou—boyfriend," Roman explained. "I'm not leaving her alone."

The other man's features softened.

"That's fine you can ride in the back of the ambulance with her."

Roman nodded in response.

"You've got to let me take her," the EMT added.

Roman nodded again.

*Damn it! He'd changed everything! What the hell went wrong?*

As usual, the ride to the hospital was silent and tense with only the steady beat of the monitors to fill the space.

"She's not going to make it," he told the male EMT when he had finished attaching Alexandra's I.V. line.

The man said nothing only continued to monitor Alexandra's vital signs which were weak at best.

"You don't have to answer that. I know what's coming next," Roman answered his own question before the man could give his opinion, an opinion he already knew.

*The ending was the same… exactly the same!*

Anxiously, he waited in North General's waiting room for only a few minutes this time, sitting on an uncomfortable plastic chair staring at the outdated eighties style pictures hanging on the walls. All the while silently mumbling a prayer… something he'd done a lot during the past few days. Lost in his thoughts, he didn't hear when the doctor came in to deliver the devastating news.

"Mr. Giordano?"

"Yes, that's me." His stomach started doing somersaults as he braced himself for the news. "I already know what happened. She had a coronary attack, right?"

The doctor looked down at his chart.

"I'm so very sorry, Mr. Giordano, but we did everything—"

"I know," Roman interrupted, not really caring if he was being rude.

"We really did do everything possible," the doctor explained.

"CPR… defibrillator… the works," he responded without heat, without emotion. His entire body started to feel cold, even though his forehead and palms were sweating.

The doctor's eyes narrowed.

"Are you alright, sir?" The man's green scrubs attracted his attention. "I think you should sit down so I can check your vitals."

"There's no need," Roman grumbled. "It's my fault… all my fault."

"It's not your fault," Dr. Reed comforted unsuccessfully. "Ms. Martin's injuries were too extensive… massive hemorrhaging and brain swelling too."

## L. D. K. Johnson

Roman felt the room move under his feet and realized he had stumbled onto his knees. As his ability to function ceased, he heard the doctor shouting for a wheelchair and a nurse.

*Kill me now. Put me out of my misery.*

"I need some help over here, Nurse Marshall!" Dr. Reed shouted over his shoulder. It was the last thing he heard before the room went black.

Roman woke on the same gurney near the nurse's station across from the waiting room, a small carton of apple juice and a carton of vanilla pudding waited for him. Looking around in a daze, the surreal nature of what had happened scratched at his soul like some wild beast. Quickly, he drank the juice, but stuck the pudding in his coat pocket. The juice was warm and tasted bitter.

Guilt ate at him like a tangible entity. Alexandria would still be alive if he hadn't made her feel like she was some pity screw. Truthfully, being with her tonight was the best night of his life. No one had ever made him feel so content.

So, needed. So, loved.

If it weren't for his inability to admit his feelings for her, she would be safe now in his apartment, cuddling in his arms, arms that now couldn't stop shaking. Alexandra would be alive, and he'd still have his best friend. There was no forgiving himself for that.

Agonizing waves of tears flowed down his face, and he let them, not caring who saw. When he could hardly see in front of him,

Roman brushed them away crossly then began to trudge pointlessly around the silent hospital passageways. Nurse Marshall saw him; her look of concern made him want to melt into the floor and disappear.

"Mr. Giordano," the woman addressed him by name, which was different, and handed him a cup of cold water from a nearby dispenser. "Are you looking for the chapel?"

Glancing up, he noticed this time he was at the sign that pointed the way to the hospital sanctuary.

"Yes," He stared down the all too familiar corridor.

"Do you want me to show you where it is?"

He shook his head.

"I know the way," Roman whispered and gave the nurse a small nod.

"The young woman who passed away was she your girlfriend?" Her tone was soft and comforting.

"Alexandra was my best friend," Roman's voice cracked with loss. "I think she was my soul mate."

The words rang true, and he felt the loss like a kick to the groin.

"I loved her," he confessed what he had already known. "I've always loved her. I just didn't realize how much until now."

Sympathetically, Nurse Marshall rested her hand on his shoulder.

"I'm so sorry for your loss," she said, and he knew it was sincere. "I'll walk with you."

The shaking in his hands lessened.

"Thank you."

"Why don't you go to the chapel? It should be empty now. Maybe saying a prayer might help you feel better. Sometimes when I've had a tough day, I like to stop in and light a candle or two. Often, it helps put things in perspective."

In complete agreement, he followed the nurse to the small chapel.

"Thank you again." She turned and began her short trek back to the nurse's station, but before she could get to the end of the hallway he called out.

"You're always so kind, Nurse Marshall."

"How do you know my name?" The woman paused.

"We've met before."

Her blue eyes narrowed with suspicion then softened.

"When I helped Dr. Reed earlier."

"Yes," Roman placated which made her relax again.

"Would you like me to stay with you for a while?" she questioned, smiling sweetly. Her bright blue eyes sparkled like sapphires, and the kindness in her face made him feel safe.

"Could you?"

She nodded her head solemnly.

"Thank you, ma'am."

"Please call me, Olivia," Olivia insisted. "And you are more than welcome."

# Four Past Midnight

Then they walked to the small chapel, and she held his hand as if he were a small child.

He briefly hesitated before going inside of the Spanish-style sanctuary. The décor of the small space was forever etched into his mind along with the muted color scheme, which was meant to soothe, had the opposite effect. Now it suffocated him. Even the aroma of the heated candle wax combined with a fresh citrus wood polish accosted his frayed nerves. During the past few days, he had prayed many times, but now it seemed more than something he was supposed to do. It felt like something he *had* to do. *Wanted* to do.

"I'm going crazy. That's the only explanation," he admitted in a hushed tone as Olivia led him farther inside, still holding his hand.

Like the previous nights, the hospital chapel was free of patrons. The pair chose a pew near the front after they had lit their candles. As they sat the heat radiating off of them reminded him that he was still damp. Slowly, he removed his trench coat and hung it over the back of the pew to dry.

"Go ahead, dear," Olivia encouraged.

"I've done this so many times I don't know what else to say," he complained.

Unable to control his emotions, tears flowed again, and he let them. Let them run down his face until his eyes burned from it. He loved Alexandra. Loved her with everything that he was. He felt the loss in his bones. Having his heart literally carved out of his chest would be more appealing than the pain he felt now.

"Say what you feel. Get it all out," she insisted. "Don't hold anything back this time."

"Huh?"

"Go on; say what's in your heart," his new friend beamed. "It'll be fine. I promise."

Finally, he knelt and closed his eyes.

"Dear father, I love Alexandra, since the day we met I've loved her. And now the thought of living without her smile… without her humor… without her touch… I can't breathe. I need her back. Give me one more chance to make it right.

"Please, give me one more chance…"

# XI

*Beep! Beep! Beep!*

Roman rolled over, grabbed the annoying clock, yanked it from the wall and threw it with all of his might. It hit the far wall, shattering into a hundred jagged pieces.

*Now that was satisfying.* With that done, he rolled over and went back to sleep.

Alexandra huffed, and then glanced at her wristwatch for the tenth time in fifteen minutes.

"Where the hell is Roman?"

He was never late. He was just as OCD as she when it came to punctuality. Losing patience, she fished her cell phone out of her purse, found his number and hit the speed dial. It rang until it went to voicemail.

"Damn it! Pick up."

Immediately, she hit the redial button and waited, her leg shaking nervously under the desk. Finally, he picked up on the sixth ring.

"What?"

"Well, good morning to you too." Relief filled her just from the sound of his voice. "Why aren't you at work?"

"I'm sick."

He really didn't sound well at all.

"I'm sorry, but what about the public works story?" she questioned, reminding him of their current assignment. "I thought we'd be working on it today."

There was a long pregnant pause that filled the space between them before he finally responded.

"I don't care about the fucking story, Alexandra," her best friend snapped. "Do what you want with it."

Now that definitely wasn't Roman.

"Roman, if you need help, like you're being held at gunpoint just say, 'I'd like a piece of red velvet cake.'"

He absolutely hated red velvet cake. He'd always say that the bright red cake made him feel queasy. She didn't understand. She loved cake in general.

"I'm not being held prisoner," he answered flatly.

"Good." She let out a relieved sigh. "What should I do about the story?"

"I told you—"

"Yes, I know what you said," she interrupted. "But that's unacceptable… Roman… Roman?"

# Four Past Midnight

The damned man hung-up on her.

*Well, that was rude!*

An hour later, there was a knock on his penthouse door.

"Go away!" Roman yelled to the faceless arm making the damn knocking sound.

"Let me in, Roman!"

*Damn it!*

He'd purposely not gone into work, trying to avoid her completely. If he wasn't near her… if he could stay in his apartment until tomorrow or at least until after four past midnight, everything would be fine. He was sure of it.

"If you don't open this door at once, I'll get the building superintendent to open it."

*Why did he introduce her to the building staff?*

"Okay, Giordano!" she bellowed. "I'm going downstairs to get—"

"Alexandra, I told you, I'm sick." He made a fake cough and then pretended to blow his nose. "You'll catch it if you come near me."

"Roman, I'm not leaving until you let me in."

*That damned stubborn woman.*

"I brought you some soup: chicken noodle with tons of vegetables and big chunks of white meat chicken. *Mmm*, I even got you some orange juice *without* the pulp, just the way you like it!"

"Shit!" He stood, dragged himself to the door and opened it without inviting her inside.

"Good morning, Mister Grumpy Pants." She studied him and made a face. "You really do look terrible."

"Thanks," he dripped sarcasm. "It's been a long few days."

When he ran his hand over his face, he felt the stubbles running amok.

"I brought everything we'll need to work from home," she said, holding up her briefcase. "All of the past interviews, photos, and the recent customer claims of price gouging. Are you ready to get to work?"

"You can't stay," he stated harshly, plopping himself down onto the leather sofa.

Bruno stopped chewing on his rawhide bone to sniff the mouth-watering aroma coming from the brown paper bag holding the soup.

"I'll be in tomorrow we can work on it then," he amended, wishing she would leave.

"No, can do, boss," she replied, taking off her yellow raincoat to reveal a pair of faded jeans, a form-fitting white t-shirt, and white sneakers.

One word came to mind: *Tasty!*

# Four Past Midnight

"The owner of the paper called this morning to talk with you about the public works write up," she paused.

"Let me guess she wants it no later than—"

She interrupted, "Noon today."

"Really?" Surprised at the change, Roman sat up, noticing the drastic changes to his day already. "That's three hours from now."

"See," she teased. "That's why you're the boss. What should I do first? I've got a lunch meeting with—"

"Macintosh, I know and another meeting with some other guy."

"You are correct," she said, eyes narrowed suspiciously. "Have you been going through my calendar again?"

He shook his head no.

"Call those clowns you're supposed to meet today and do phone interviews instead, so we can make the deadline."

"Good idea." She smiled in agreement.

The truth of the matter was he didn't want any man touching his woman's ass or asking her out. Wait! *His woman... well, damn it!* He was her first, after all, even if technically that awesome sexual encounter was null and void, but he planned to fix that.

Sitting straighter, he switched to work mode.

"I know exactly what we're gonna do. First..."

## L. D. K. Johnson

Noon, on the dot, Roman faxed the owner of the paper the final write-up. Alexandra wasn't surprised when she gave him the thumbs up to run the story in today's late edition. The satisfaction of finishing a story always pleased her. Not the needing a cigarette kind of satisfied, but the kind that called for an extra-large chocolate chip muffin.

Tired and hungry, she blew out a low, steady whistle, cracked her neck in a very unladylike fashion and then announced, "I guess my work here is done. I'm going home to vegetate on my couch."

Her best friend who sat at the dining table looked up from his notes.

"We haven't had lunch yet."

"I'll make a sandwich when I get home," she informed with a smile. "Right now, all I need is my favorite jammies and my remote control—"

His emerald eyes twinkled suggestively.

"I meant the remote control for my television. *Pervert!*"

They both laughed.

"You should stay," he suggested, reaching for the paper bag holding the soup. "I'll share."

How could she turn that offer down.

# Four Past Midnight

The soup was delicious, as always. The Sweetshop Café never disappointed.

"So," she said, gathering their bowls and spoons. "When did this fake flu come on?"

"This morning." He stilled knowing she'd just caught him in a lie.

"Uh-huh," she snickered, knowing he knew that she knew. She'd caught him lying to other people before, but he'd never lied to her. "Don't worry, I won't rat you out to the boss."

"Thank you so much," he met her sarcasm, and raised her an arched brow. "Do you wanna watch a rerun of Forever Knight?"

He knew that would make her stay, and he really wanted her to stay. Truth of the matter was… *he really, really* wanted to get her naked and on his bed again, but most of all he wanted to know that she was safe.

"Why?" her tone hushed, those sultry baby browns narrowed, resembling those of a seasoned prosecutor interrogating a criminal. "You hate that show."

He shook his head.

"Since when do you watch Nick?"

"Since last night," he confessed.

"What did you think of it?"

The guilty man hung his head in mock shame.

"*Aha!*" she yelled loudly. "I knew if you gave it a chance, you'd like it. It's only taken nine years, but you've evolved into a rerun connoisseur. I'm proud of you, Roman."

Using the back of her hand, she wiped away an invisible tear of joy.

"Be quiet," he chuckled under his breath, his overly long hair spilling over his lovely, dark-lashed eyes. "Do you want to watch an episode or not? I recorded it."

"I wanna be La Croix when I grow up," Alexandra announced to the living room in general.

"You're a woman—"

"Really? Finally noticed, huh?" Her words were teasing as she poked him with her finger on his bicep.

Without warning, he leaned forward, leaving less than a foot between them, his breath warm against her skin and fragranced with a hint of citrus. The sweet scent did strange things to her lower body.

A knowing smile graced his lips as he stared into her eyes.

"I've noticed for quite a while now."

Slowly, he inched toward her. Ignoring the fact his words had caused her mouth to fall open and her eyes to bulge out of their sockets.

"I'm attracted to you."

# Four Past Midnight

*There he said it!*

"I was worried about telling you," he wholeheartedly admitted. "But now I want you to know."

"Hold on a minute." His friend stood suddenly and walked over to the breakfast bar, putting at least twenty feet between them. Her mind racing as she pondered what he had said.

"Where is this coming from?"

"It shouldn't be a surprise."

He followed like a jungle cat stalking a helpless doe.

"We spend a lot of time together, work and private. We enjoy the same things. We laugh at the same corny jokes… *and*…" he continued, stopping directly in front of her, chest to nose, before adding, "I find you incredibly… *hot*."

The squeal of laughter that erupted from Alexandra's chest shocked them both. Roman's seductive face—she guessed it was his seductive face—morphed into a look of confusion. His jaw clenched, the vein at his right temple throbbed, and a steeled expression crawled across his features.

"What's so funny?" he finally asked after she had stopped snorting with amusement.

"You."

She pressed her lips together in an attempt to stifle the laughter that had turned into a fit of giggles and snorts. Roman, on the other hand, his brows arched all the way up to his hairline.

"You've always treated me like a younger sister," Alexandra declared as she attempted to quell her fit. "Never, have you looked at me like *this*."

"There's a first time for everything," he announced, bending his head, angling it so their lips were in position, and went in for the kill or in this case… a kiss.

Another snicker escaped from her making him pull back. All he could do was stare at her in disbelief.

"This can't be happening," he mumbled then angrily walked back to the living room and plopped down onto the sofa.

"I'm sorry." She sat on a nearby barstool. "You can't expect me to fall into your big, muscular arms because you want me to, because all of sudden you think I'm… *hot*."

"Why not?" Roman questioned. "You're attracted to me. Don't deny it."

She swallowed hard and then explained.

"I won't deny it," she proudly revealed. "I've had feelings for you since the day you took down Bobby Lieberman. No. That's not true. I've liked you since the day I saw you in the front office registering for school."

His eyes widened at her confession and a blush stole over his handsome, rugged features.

"Why do you think I volunteered to tutor you?" she grinned roguishly.

"I always thought you just liked to study," he replied, feeling like a big dork.

"Yeah, right," the amused reporter smirked. "I would have given my right arm to be with you. Tutoring was the best vehicle to make that happen."

"I had no idea," he admitted as she shrugged her shoulders. "Why didn't you ever tell me how you felt?"

"Are you kidding?" Alexandra rolled her eyes. "The school nerd—a-k-a *Alexander* Martin—in love with the quarterback of the football team and the most popular kid at school. This isn't an ABC Family teen drama, Roman. It's real life."

"You should have told me," he said, shaking his dark locks.

"You should have figured it out," she fired back, all humor draining from her face. "All of the signs were there."

"What signs?"

Anger bubbled to the surface ready to spew out of her like *Mt. Vesuvius* and Roman Giordano was *Pompeii*.

"You are the densest man on the face of the planet." She threw her hands in the air in frustration as he sat staring at her like she was possessed. "I've supported you emotionally since the first day we met. I tutored you to the point of getting you a scholarship to your first-choice college. I went to every football game in high school to cheer you on even though I hate football. I'd prefer having a root canal done."

"Okay, I get it," he glared at her.

"No. I don't think you do." She took another deep breath. "I've sat around for years watching you go through half the women on the

East Coast. All of them tall, leggy, gorgeous, bubbleheads with ginormous gazongas—"

"Gazongas?" He snickered.

She shot him with a fatal stare, and he shut up immediately.

"I've been patient," Alexandra declared. "Holding out hope that one day you'd open your eyes and see what was waiting right in front of you."

"But you never told me," he accused, his temper getting the better of him.

"I was being subtle," she sighed.

"I'm a man, Alexandra!" he shouted, that vein running a marathon on his temple. "I don't understand *subtle*. If you wanted me to know you liked me then, damn it, woman, you've got to tell me."

"What should I have done?" she huffed. "Break into your apartment, strip down to my underwear, drape myself over the bed, and let you have your wicked way with me?"

"That would have been a good start," he blurted. "I'd prefer if you lose the underwear."

"Ugg!"

That was it. Before he could stop her, she grabbed her briefcase and rain jacket and made a beeline for the front door. She almost tripped over Bruno in the process, when the nervous dog stepped into her path stumbling over its own paws to avoid being stepped on.

# Four Past Midnight

"Don't go! Wait a minute, Alexandra!" Roman looked down, relieved that this time he was wearing his pajama bottoms and a gray t-shirt. "We're not finished!"

"I am." Her hand now on the doorknob ready to bolt as she added, "We've known each other for nine years. Nine years, Roman. We've worked together for almost a year. Our families have spent countless holidays and vacations together—"

"Alexandra," he soothed, holding up his hands in surrender as she began pacing the length of the foyer. "Calm down. Don't be so emotional."

She stopped, dead in her tracks and stared at the giant demigod looking out of his element and endearingly gorgeous at the same time. Bewildered, he stared back at her.

"Don't be so emotional?" she hacked out as if she were choking on the words.

Roman continued to stare, afraid to speak.

"Don't be so emotional. Is that what you said?" Her blood was boiling, and she hoped she wouldn't have a coronary or a stroke. "I'm leaving."

"I'm not gonna chase after you if you leave."

He leaned against the wall, giving her the most *'I-don't-give-a-shit'* expression he could muster, although he felt anything but that. He wanted her to stay more than he wanted his next breath.

Then out of nowhere those dreaded words rushed past her full, pouty lips.

"I love you, Roman."

The declaration battered his ears like a sledgehammer hitting concrete.

"Are you happy now?"

Surprised, he stood stock still.

"There!" she barked. "I've told you… point blank. I'm in love with you, Roman. Totally and completely."

Afraid to move. Afraid to blink. His head began to swim.

"Did you hear me? I said, *I love you*."

"I heard you," he whispered like they were in a confessional, and he was a priest.

"Well?" Her eyes narrowed and her foot began to tap the floor in frustration.

"Well… what?"

*Say it.*

He heard the words in his mind.

*Say it, damn it… before she leaves… again. Tell her that you love her.*

Folding her arms across her chest, she asked, "Would you like to say anything to me?"

*He tried to say it, but the words got stuck in his throat.*

"About what?" He wasn't trying to be dense; he really was dense.

*Say it now.*

"Ugg!"

# Four Past Midnight

She ran out of the apartment, into the hallway and pressed the button for the elevator, rage replacing her unshed tears.

"I quit!" She spat the words out like a viper spits venom.

"You can't be serious," he condemned, looking down at his bare feet.

*Where the hell did he put his shoes?*

"You bet your ass I am," Alexandra hissed, pressing the button again.

"You can't quit your job."

Without warning, the realization hit him. He had to tell her the truth before she left him... again. He did love her. He really did. He opened his mouth to say just that, but instead he said:

"You're under contract. I could sue you for the violation of... of..." His disloyal mind went blank.

*Fucking tongue had a mind of its own.*

"Then sue me," she challenged, practically daring him to do it. "I don't give a rat's ass. You can kiss my ass for all I care. It's all the same to me."

"If you come back inside, I can definitely kiss your ass," he joked, trying to lighten the mood, but the sexy as hell woman wouldn't listen.

"Goodbye, Roman," she stated flatly as the bell sounded letting them know the elevator had finally arrived.

Quickly, she stepped into the small space, pushed the lobby button, and stared at her shoes, and then Alexandra Martin said the worse thing anyone could say to another person.

"I hope you have a good life, Roman." And with those words hanging over his head like the blade of a guillotine, she was gone.

*Chase after her, damn it!*

Knowing that he had to, he sprinted back into the apartment, past a very irritated Bruno, down the hallway, and finally to his bedroom, where his sneakers were hiding under the bed mocking him... again. As fast as he could, he donned the irritating footwear, and then grabbed the windbreaker that was hanging over by the closet door.

*Keys! Keys! Where the hell were his keys?*

Ah ha!

He ran back to the foyer and sitting on the console tabletop were his keys. They were probably in cahoots with his shoes and pants from the night before.

Mindfully, he glanced at the digital display on the living room DVR. It was only a few minutes past one in the afternoon, but he still cursed a blue streak.

"Fucking woman... had to leave... damned sonofabitch... not again... please... not again," he rambled trying to get his feet to move faster.

He ran back to the elevator, pushed the down-button, and impatiently waited.

# Four Past Midnight

"Fuck this shit!" He ran to the emergency stairwell and flew down over ten flights of stairs until he made it to the empty lobby. A crowd had gathered outside near the front of the building.

"Fuck it all to hell!" He pushed past all of the people, the crowd thick with onlookers, all wide-mouthed and grumbling frantically. Then a familiar face came into focus. It was George.

"Mr. Giordano!"

The man was laughing and clutching his cell phone, his knuckles white from the force.

"This is the actor who played *Commander Warf* on *Star Trek Deep Space Nine*," he tried to explain, tears of joy welling at the corner of his blue eyes.

George was his biggest fan.

"He's going to be moving into the building! Isn't that incredible?"

"Alexandra?" Roman panted; the word choppy as he tried to catch his breath.

He had to start going back to the gym more than three times a week or stop eating chocolate chip muffins with his friend. Nah! He'd take the former. He enjoyed listening to Alexandra eat her muffin, moaning as she savored each decadent bite. The memories making his cock spring to life.

"I think I saw her heading toward the subway," George informed as he waited patiently as *Michael Dorn*, the famous *Mr. Warf*, signed autographs.

Roman pushed forward another step, looked up and down the busy sidewalk, and felt a surge of disbelief wash over him. To his relief, the amazing woman of his dreams was not on the pavement where she lay earlier with her eyes half open staring up at him.

*Hallelujah!*

There was still a chance to fix this!

Hastily, he made his way back to his apartment with a wide grin. There was no way he was going to let the insufferable rookie get away from him now. Not when there was light at the end of his very long tunnel.

Alexandra was going to listen to him if it was the last thing he did.

# XII

"Arrogant… clueless… brainless! No, he isn't brainless! He is very intelligent."

She shook her head. Damn! She couldn't even insult him properly.

*Freaking Roman Giordano!*

Dropping her briefcase on the floor beside the hallway table, she kicked off her sensible white sneakers as she walked to the small galley-style kitchen that was much too small to be considered practical. Angrier than she'd ever been before, she yanked open the freezer door and fished out the emergency half pint of *Ben and Jerry's Chunky Monkey* ice cream that she kept hidden behind a container of *Tofutti* fat-free, non-dairy, ice milk.

Automatically, she went to the living room, turned on the television, and found her favorite episode of *Forever Knight.*

By this time, she realized her jeans were cutting off her circulation.

*Damn it!*

She really needed to join a gym, but that was tomorrow's problem. Frantically, she removed the offending garment throwing them on the floor next to the small loveseat then sat on the furniture in only her t-shirt and panties. Right now, the only thing she wanted to do was drown her sorrows in a tub of creamy, cold, deliciousness.

*Flabby tummy be damned!*

Then a thought came to her as she practically ripped the lid off of the small container. She'd just cursed out her boss and quit her job. *Hell!* How was she going to pay rent? How was she going to keep the utilities on? It was almost winter, and she'd freeze to death without electricity. She didn't want to die alone in her small yet charming studio.

*Damn that Roman!*

Living in Soho, a neighborhood located south of Houston Street in Lower Manhattan was an eclectic chick's dream come true. The area, known for its numerous artists' lofts and art galleries, and for the wide variety of shops ranging from trendy boutiques to outlets of upscale national and international chain stores, spoke to her on a spiritual level.

The neighborhood where she lived was comprised of several pre-war buildings in the heart of the district. With apartments that were intended to match the historic details of the area and offered contemporary conveniences in a practical yet chic locale. It was no wonder the rent was so high.

Looking around, she grinned. It really was a very charming little space. It had high industrial ceilings adorned with exposed iron beams, accent walls with the original red brick, and recessed halogen lighting accentuating the historic architecture of the early 1900's. The apartment itself was one large space with only the bathroom and closets completely enclosed.

Other than those two rooms, her place was an open floor plan.

# Four Past Midnight

The only problem that she could see was the historic building still had a few hidden problems to contend with, such as needing an entire plumbing overhaul. Other than that, it was a home fit for a queen. Not to mention with a price tag to match.

*Shit!* She remembered she'd just quit her job. *Freaking Roman!*

Diving in with her extra-large spoon, she began shoveling the sweet, cold concoction into her mouth, regretting it after the third brain-freeze. What was she going to do? Move back to Florida and live with her parents until she died of old age.

"Grr!"

*Knock! Knock! Knock!*

*Who the hell could that be? It better not be—*

"Roman," she snarled below her breath, glaring through the peephole. The handsome face staring back made her nether regions quiver even though she was furious with him.

Flinging open the door she growled.

"I have nothing to say to you, so save your breath."

"I don't want you to quit," his words rushed past his lips in an almost incoherent stream.

Suddenly, he smiled. The small action illuminated his features making her heartbeat accelerate. And the way he looked in a pair of faded jeans, black sweater, black leather jacket, and Timberland boots should be a crime.

"Whatever."

She slammed the door in his face but forgot to relock it. Without her permission, the irritating, 6'4" Italian demigod stormed in, closing the door himself and turned the deadbolt to seal them inside.

"I didn't invite you in." Her hands clenched tightly at her sides. "Get out!"

"No, not until we hammer this out," he spoke calmly.

"I have nothing left to say," Alexandra sneered, and suddenly he lost his charming smile.

"I have plenty to say."

He took off his coat and shoes, which was one of her rules. No walking on her new floors with dirty shoes. She smiled to herself, but hardened her expression when he looked back at her.

"Fine." She went back to the loveseat and picked up the half-eaten container of ice cream.

Roman stood staring at her with his mouth hanging open and a look on his face that she'd never seen before.

"Why are you staring at me like that?" Alexandra snapped gruffly.

He cleared his throat once, twice, and then a third time before he informed in a raspy voice, "Y-you're not wearing any…" He waved at her lower region; his face flushed. "… pants."

*"Crap!"*

Alexandra flew off the loveseat, bolted toward her bedroom and quickly donned her white, terry-cloth robe before returning. When she returned, she couldn't look him in the eyes.

"Go ahead." Her head bent as she memorized the groves of the hardwood floors. "Say what you came here to say then leave."

"I've liked you since the day Bobby Lieberman tried to tackle you," Roman stated in a calm yet hushed voice.

She knew her mouth had dropped to the floor, but she couldn't be bothered to close it.

"Actually, I think I liked you when I saw you hiding in the bushes with your camera at my house trying to catch me without a shirt," he chuckled.

"I was practicing my detective skills and you were new to the neighborhood," she lied, trying to cover-up her guilt.

"Sure." He snickered.

"I got the shot, didn't I?" the woman countered.

"Only because I let you," he informed matter-of-factly. "Why would I go outside in the middle of January in just my basketball shorts?"

"I don't know," she squeaked, blushing uncontrollably. "You had just moved from New York. I figured the temperature didn't bother you."

Roman laughed, eyes glistening under the halogen lights.

"I was freezing my gonads off."

She couldn't help laughing then too.

"Why did you do it?"

"Because I'd seen you at the bus stop and you didn't have any friends and you kept staring at me like I was a piece of apple pie."

She wanted to melt into the floor and not in a good way.

"To tell you the truth, I felt sorry for you."

Her lips thinned into a hard, angry line.

"At first."

"At first?" Alexandra repeated, voice shaky.

"After you started tutoring me, I started liking you more," Roman confessed. "Not as a girlfriend, but as a friend I could say anything to, and do anything without feeling embarrassed. I could be completely myself. I didn't have to worry about being the captain of the football team with you, or if my clothes were name brand or not, because you didn't care about superficial things like that."

"Really?" she gulped, finally looking up.

Roman nodded.

"After that, I felt so comfortable with you that I did consider you like a sister."

"Great!" she groaned. "I've always wanted you to confess that to me."

"Be quiet," he ordered with a grin, stepping forward and placing a finger on her lips.

The tingles began again, and they were screaming for him to touch somewhere more south.

"I'm still talking, Miss Martin."

## Four Past Midnight

She nodded as he continued.

"It wasn't until a few days ago that you stopped being my best friend and started being *more*."

*"More?"* The one simple word filled her with hope.

"During my *déjà vu*... thing," he explained. "I kept losing you and every time you came back to me, I noticed more and more details about you, about us."

"Clarify," she begged.

Nervously, Roman cleared his throat again.

"I've always seen you, but I didn't really *see you*."

"Huh?"

Without warning, he reached up and traced his finger along the curve of her cheek, down to her slightly parted lips, then back up to tuck a stray lock of hair behind her ear.

"I began to see all the unique things that make you perfect. Your expressive brown eyes that can see straight through my bullshit," he snickered. "I noticed your full lips curve slightly at the corners whenever you say my name. It's very sexy I might add."

Alexandra blushed at his observations.

Finally, he took her hands in his and held them like they were fragile and precious.

"Continue," she smiled then added. "I'm not convinced yet."

"I noticed the lovely dimple at the curve of your ass right below you left ass cheek."

She gasped at the very personal fact and tried to step away, but he grabbed her by the waist and hauled her body against his. The feel of something big and hard poked her in the stomach causing her eyes to widen to the size of puff pastries.

"How do you know about my dimple?" she grilled, grabbing the hem of her robe and pulling it further down, trying to hide the not-so secret dimple.

Ignoring her question, he continued.

"I also know that when you are really nervous you hold your breath. That one makes me a little nervous. You'll pass out if you're not careful," he chastised, giving the tip of her nose a little tweak.

Her cheeks were on fire now and not in a good way. She wanted to run to her bathroom, shut the door and never come out.

"How the hell do you know all of this?"

"I've told you before. It's been an interesting few days."

Then slowly he leaned over and rested his forehead against hers, staring at her, green eyes to brown.

"The crazy *déjà vu*... thing?" her voice a whisper like it was a secret.

He nodded his head and the scent of citrus bath gel, and his unique scent made her swoon.

*It's now or never.*

"I love you, Alexandra," Roman declared. "I love everything about you, even your deep-seeded obsession with Forever Knight and chocolate-chip muffins. I love it all. I've been an idiot for not telling you sooner."

There was a long, agonizing moment of silence before she finally spoke.

"It's about time."

He laughed.

"I was trying to be romantic, and you've ruined the moment."

"No, the moment is perfect," she giggled. "Tell me, what else did you notice?"

"I also noticed," he divulged as he kissed a trail from her left earlobe to the shallow divot at the base of her neck, "when you come," he licked the indent with the tip of his tongue, "your entire, luscious body stiffens like a board, and you make the most erotic noises imaginable."

With that, he claimed her lips with soft, feathery touches. The barely-there motion drove her libido into high gear and all she could think of was getting him naked on her fold-out, queen-sized sleeper sofa. In response to her unspoken request, his cock nudged her again.

"That feels really—" The sudden realization that the sex-god in front of her wanted... *more*, made her panic. "Stop, Roman."

"I don't think I can." He ran both hands over her hips, circling around to her back, landing squarely on her butt.

"Why not?" Her breath started coming in choppy pants reminding her of Bruno.

"Because I've had you before."

Alexandra glared with indignation, nostrils flaring as she tried unsuccessfully to push at his highly sculpted chest.

"You certainly have not!" she objected loudly.

"Yesterday. At. My. Place." He punctuated each word with a nudge of his erection against her stomach. It felt as if a python was trying to escape from his jeans.

Before she denied his claim again, he bent brushing his lips to hers, but this time more aggressively. The plump flesh of her tantalizing mouth pressed firmly against his made his cock harden a little more. Several seconds later he slowly pulled away, watching as she opened her eyes. He gazed into weepy, brown eyes, wide with shock and his heart began to pound inside of his chest.

With a shaking hand, she touched her lips.

"What are you doing?"

"I'm kissing you, trying to change your mind about stopping." He swallowed what little moisture he had left in his mouth, lips burning to be against hers again. "Please, don't make me stop. I mean if you want me to I will, but if it were up to me—"

She giggled the sound going straight to his groin.

"You're rambling," she stated sweetly. "You never ramble."

"I want you, Alexandra," Roman blurted against his better judgment. "I want you so much I hurt from it."

She rolled her eyes, smiling.

"How can I refuse such a romantic request?" Her sarcasm noted but ignored.

"Is that a yes then?" he hoped as he squeezed her bottom.

A long pregnant moment passed as she pondered his words. Their bodies still pressed together in that incredible way. One of her hands against his chest holding him at bay while the other still pressed to her mouth.

When he thought she'd push him away she surprised him once again by reaching up, entwining her arms around his neck and pulling him down to her. The feather-light touch of her lips made him shiver. Letting her take the lead, she devoured his mouth with gentle nips, luxurious glides and sensuous licks. His entire body began to shake.

"I guess we could try," she said on a breathy whisper.

With all of the strength he could muster, he gathered her up in his arms. He wanted her so badly he could barely think. Barely complete a sentence. All he could manage to say was, "Bed, now."

Alexandra held on tight as Roman carried her to her fold out sofa in the far corner of the studio, their mouths still pressed firmly together.

"Roman?" she mumbled against his lips.

"What is it, Sunshine?"

"I'm still a, you know." She felt herself being lowered to the floor in front of the tasteful floral sleeper.

"I realize that," he confirmed, snapping out of his lust-filled thoughts.

"Does that put a kink in your devilish plan to seduce me?"

She kind of hoped it did. A wave of uncertainty was lapping at her ankles threatening to turn into a twenty-foot tidal wave. He smiled, eyes twinkling mischievously.

"I see."

Instead, he kissed her again, a sweet, patient kiss that eased the nervous pit that was forming in her stomach.

"Do you trust me, Sunshine?"

"I do, but with you kissing me like that, I'm having a hard time being sensible."

Chuckling he commanded, "Undress me."

The low, animalistic sound made her sex clench in an almost painful way.

"Why do I have to undress you?" She didn't want to tell him her hands were shaking so badly that she didn't think she could perform the simple task.

"I'm begging you."

He bent again, but this time instead of claiming her lips he sucked on her earlobe. The steady suctioning motion made her almost forget her own name. *My God!* If he could make her feel so out of control with only a suck on her lobe—what could he do to her when he really got started?

Suddenly, she really wanted to know the extent of his sexual prowess.

"Okay, if you insist."

# Four Past Midnight

"Get me naked," he growled against her ear. "I'm gonna burst if you don't get this show on the road."

Gathering all of her courage, she began stripping off his unwanted clothing. First, grabbing the hem of his sweater and quickly pulling it up his yummy torso, letting her eyes drink in all of his attributes: rock hard pecs, indecently wicked abs, tapered waist and the sexiest trail of jet-black hair. Her hands roamed freely enjoying every line, nook, and cranny. Finally, she reached the waistband of his jeans and paused.

"You've gotten to the best part," he smirked, enjoying her innocence. "Don't stop now."

Accepting his challenge, she unbuckled his belt, pulling it through the loops and letting it fall to the floor, the buckle making a loud clank. Next, came the button. *Good grief!* The button. She held her breath as she undid the cool metal fastener. Then she was at the zipper, taking a deep breath she slowly pulled it downward, her hands beginning to shake uncontrollably.

"Are you alright?" Roman's strong fingers were kneading her backside like a piece of dough.

"I'm not sure," she mumbled. "I don't know what the hell I'm doing. I know you've had a lot of experience and I don't want to disappoint you."

He grinned, using his thumb and forefinger to angle her head up. The acceptance of her in every way shone in his emotion-filled eyes.

"You could never disappoint me." He gave her a chaste kiss on the forehead. The sweet gesture made her heart leap in her chest. "I'm just glad you're letting me have the honor."

Those words were her undoing, spurring her on to seize the moment.

"We can't have sex with clothes on, right?"

"Well, technically you can if—"

She grimaced and he immediately held his tongue and then spoke more cautiously.

"But usually, no, clothes just get in the way."

No more words were spoken as she shoved his jeans down his muscular legs, leaving only his black boxer briefs on. She couldn't contain the gasp that escaped her chest as he stood staring down at her like a man ready to get down to business. So-to-speak.

The Roman god Jupiter came to mind as he stood waiting to be devoured. High regal cheekbones, straight nose, soft, sensuous full mouth, black inky locks hanging loosely over one emerald eye in that all too sexy gaze, and muscles rippling and flexing every time he took a breath. Her eyes wandered further down his torso, over his well-defined eight pack, down his lean, tapered hips, to the trail of black hair that led from his bellybutton down to his—

"Holy! Moly!" she gasped when her eyes made contact with the massive bulge currently trying to break free of his underwear. He was the epitome of sex! Glorious and wild and passion-filled and he wanted her.

A soft chuckle brought her back to the scene currently playing out before her.

"You're gonna make me blush if you keep eyeing my goodies that way."

"Well, I guess what I'm about to do is really gonna make you blush," she said, just as she hooked her thumbs into the cotton fabric of his boxer briefs and slid them over his hips, down his muscular thighs, along his perfectly shaped legs until the garment pooled at his feet.

"Step out," she ordered.

Her breath came in soft pants as she realized she was at eye level with a very long, very thick, very angry looking cock. The sight of it made her hungry for a taste, so she tasted. Leaning forward she graced the tip of his cock with a long, wet swipe, stopping momentarily to look up at his flushed face, his chest heaving like he'd just run the Boston Marathon.

"More," he hissed through gritted teeth, large, strong hands cupped her cheek.

"Mmm," she hummed, taking the entire mushroom shaped head into her hot mouth, using her tongue to rub circles right below the tip. Roman's entire body stiffened, his hips gently rocking encouraging her to take a little—

*"More."* His head tilted backward, and his eyes squeezed shut.

Boldly, she grasped him at the base of his very impressive almost scary erection. Her fingers were unable to close completely around it and took a couple of inches into her eager mouth. Slowly, she worked his impossibly hard shaft. In and out. Up and down. His soft moans causing liquid arousal to pool in her anxious sex.

"That feels amazing." He watched as his member disappeared into Alexandra's virgin mouth. The idea he was the only one to be *here* made his chest swell with male pride.

"You taste delicious, Roman." She stopped momentarily, her eyes glistening with emotion.

"Enough," he growled, pulling her to a standing position. His emerald eyes, darker than she'd ever seen them before. "I think it's time to get you naked, Sunshine."

Alexandra's mind went into a state of high alert, her blood pressure increasing to the point of giving her a slight headache. She was playing with fire. Roman was no stranger to seduction. With him, foreplay always… *always*… led to sex. He had boasted many times that he'd never heard a woman say no.

"Roman." She swallowed what remaining moisture she could before adding, "I've never had sex, remember?"

That did it. The corners of his mouth turned down transforming his face into a studious expression. She could see the wheels turning and was certain he was hatching up a plan to divest her of her innocence.

"I don't know if it's gonna fit. I'm pretty sure it won't," she reasoned.

"I know it fits," he reassured. "Your body stretches."

The look she gave told him she didn't quite believe him.

Nervously, Alexandra began clenching her fingers to give them something to do.

"I don't know."

For a long moment he stood, looking at her from different angles, and then asked, "Could you get a towel from the bathroom?"

# Four Past Midnight

Her uncertainty showed, but she left disappearing into the nearby bathroom. Several minutes past as she debated whether or not to follow through with Roman's request for... *more*. As she stood in a state of confusion searching her linen closet for a towel, she saw her reflection in the mirror. This would be the last time she'd look at herself as a...

"Alexandra?" Roman's deep, sultry voice brought her back to reality. The impatience in his voice caused her palms to sweat. "What's taking so long?"

"I-I'm coming," she yelled back.

"If you don't get your fine ass in here, you won't be," he said with a chuckle.

She couldn't help rolling her eyes.

"And stop rolling your eyes at me," he added with a laugh from behind the closed door.

*He knew her so well.*

Another moment had passed before she returned holding a soft, thick bath towel. The sight before her made any doubt that Roman wanted this to be special leave her mind.

"What have you done?" she asked with trembling lips.

Her living room looked like a scene from a *Harlequin* romance with lighted pillar candles scattered throughout the small space, giving the room a dream-like glow. Her comforter was on the floor next to the sleeper sofa with her special occasion black satin sheet over it.

"Why are we on the floor?" Alexandra giggled.

The man of her dreams frowned, giving her one of his patented pouts, his expression priceless.

"Your mattress in too short, half of my legs were dangling over the edge. It was too uncomfortable."

He grinned and the expression transformed his face into a work of art, something you'd see painted on a canvas and hanging at the *Louvre* in Paris.

Her heart clenched at his thoughtfulness.

"I see," she purred.

"Do you like it?"

The heated look he gave made her knees shake.

*Holy crap! This was really happening!*

"I love it. It's perfect."

And it really was.

"Great," he said on a sigh.

Finally, her commonsense kicked in, proving she wasn't a complete moron.

"What about protection?"

"I know we don't need protection," he informed, noting her surprised reaction to his words and her forehead crinkled with confusion. "You're on the pill."

Alexandra's brow hitched just a bit before he clarified.

"You have really terrible cramps during your period. The doctor prescribed them to help manage the pain."

A bewildered expression suddenly washed over her face, and he took a deep cleansing breath before he spoke.

"I told you; we've had this conversation before."

"Huh," she replied with a frown. "But—"

"But what?" His impressive arms folded across his chest.

Her upper lip began to perspire, but she had to speak her mind.

"I know I'm clean, but you've—"

"I get tested every six months and I haven't had sex with anyone in a year," he reassured.

"Alright," she contemplated, trying to stall the determined man currently sizing her up like a side of prime rib. "Do you know what you're doing with someone like me?"

"I've told you before… we've already had sex… last night… I mean… on that alternate day…"

She stared at him like he'd just escaped the loony bin.

"Obviously, since the day reset, you're a virgin again," he grinned, earning him a steely scowl. "But I promise to be as gentle as I possibly can, okay?"

She nodded her consent.

"Do you think it's gonna hurt?" The concerned expression on his face was the only answer she got.

*Great!*

Holding out his hand, he tugged her closer. The scent of heavily aroused male flooded her senses.

"No more stalling. I need you naked."

Reaching down he untied the sash of her robe, pushing the soft material off of her shoulders. The garment silently fell to the floor. Slowly, he grabbed the hem of her t-shirt and inched it over her hips, mid-drift, torso, chest, finally yanking it up and over her head. Then he tossed it away like a piece of used tissue somewhere behind the sleeper sofa.

With her almost naked, his gaze drifted over her in a heated caress until it landed on her heaving breasts.

"I've been dreaming about these," he informed with an air of awe that made her breath hitch in her throat.

With deft fingers, he undid the front clasp of her bra, allowing the garment to fall aside exposing her completely to his fiery gaze.

"You're beautiful," he praised with a heavy sigh. "Not too big, but more than a handful."

Gently, he reached out and ran the back of his hand over her right breast then turned his hand, so his palm came to cup the heavy mound, his slightly calloused thumb making small circles over her tightly beaded nipple. She closed her eyes trying to keep herself from fainting. No one had ever touched her like this before and she wondered why. It felt so *naughty*.

Without hesitation, he leaned down and blew over the peak making it harden to the point of pain. Before she could protest, he lowered his mouth and took the point into his hot, wet mouth. His tongue drew invisible circles over it until she thought she'd scream from it.

"*Mmm,*" he growled, the vibrations sending need from the point where he teased her, down to her womb, finally pooling in her now soaking sex. She squeezed her thighs together to keep from spontaneously combusting. "Your nipples get so hard when I do this. So… damn… hard."

With a loud, wet *pop*, he released the aching bud and found its twin, lavishing the other nipple with just as much vigor as the first. Her legs really did buckle then, but Roman encircled her waist and held her securely in place with two strong hands. The subtle scent of his body wash filled her mind with more lustful thoughts.

"You're trembling," Roman stated matter-of-factly when her breathing had stopped. He frowned. "Alexandra, if you hold your breath, you're gonna faint, and then I'll have to take you while you're unconscious."

Her lips parted to swear at his comment, but he sealed his mouth over hers before she could call him whatever dreadful thing that had come to mind.

This time he was in complete control doing wicked things to her. He licked and nipped and explored every part of the space leaving nothing to the imagination at the things he could do to her with that talented pink muscle. When she thought she couldn't take anymore, he sought out her tongue and sucked the tip into his mouth. The constant pulling action made her clit begin to pulse to an almost painful beat.

It was both heaven and hell.

"Roman, you're driving me crazy." She heard the words, but didn't recognize who said it, the raspy sound of her own voice sounding foreign to her ears.

Chuckling seductively, he whispered, "Just enjoy it."

His words ignited her desire as he took her hand and guided it to his hard-as-iron member.

"I need you to touch me. When you touch me, I know that this will all be okay."

She waited, not sure exactly what he wanted her to do. Sensing her unease, he took her hand and placed it directly on top of his cock.

"I-I don't know what to do," her words jumbled as she stared down at her hand holding his cock like it was a poisonous snake getting ready to strike.

"Do what feels natural," he replied, then kissed her forehead.

Alexandra touched him *there*, but her hands stilled as he began to circle his hips, rubbing his cock against her slightly sweaty palm. He didn't seem to mind as he allowed her to touch his shaft.

"Up and down… not too hard, yeah, perfect."

The feel of steel encased in silk was a sensation that sent her mind into overdrive. His throaty moans of pleasure spurred her on to move lower until she held his heavy balls in her hand.

"Lightly run your fingernails over them. *Mmm*, that feels really good."

Moving to the side of her neck, he adjusted his head to get a better angle. Starting right below her left ear, he began a slow trail of wet kisses that made their way south across her graceful neck down to her collarbone. She jumped when he gently nipped her skin, and then swiped his tongue over the area to soothe the sting.

"You like that don't you?" Roman prompted. "Don't be shy. Not with me, Alexandra."

"Yes," she replied on a low, raspy moan.

He continued his wicked ministrations.

"You surprised me," her whispered answer seemed loud in the stillness of the studio. Their heavy breathing echoed around the cozy well decorated space. "But it feels incredible. Please, don't stop."

He laughed before informing, "I couldn't stop even if I wanted to and believe me, I don't want to."

Moving lower, he kissed a trail down the valley between her breasts, continuing further over the sensitive skin of her torso, abdomen, and finally... *finally*... he dropped to his knees and landed directly over her material-covered mound.

"Wait," she ordered, looking down at him with a nervous expression. "I've never liked the idea of someone doing... *that*... to me. It's so—"

"Unsanitary," he interjected sarcastically with a roll of his eyes. "I know. I know. You've mentioned it to me before."

"Stop finishing my sentences," she chastised. "It's starting to aggravate me."

He laughed again, stopping abruptly when her expression changed to an annoyed glare.

"Let me have a little taste. If you don't like how it feels, I'll stop."

She contemplated his words for a couple of seconds then nodded her consent.

Reaching up he hooked his thumbs into the black lacey fabric of her panties and slowly drew them down her slender legs. Alexandra wasn't a tall woman, 5'4" to be exact, but she had long, lovely legs for someone her height. He stopped for a moment to run his palms over the silky skin admiring the smoothness of them.

"Pick your feet up, Sunshine," he requested when the strip of fabric gathered at her ankles. She did what she was told without hesitation. "Widen your legs a little more for me. Good girl, that's perfect."

"Roman?"

"Yeah?"

"If it's alright with you," she paused, her breathing slightly irregularly making him worry that she'd faint. "Could I lie down. I don't want to collapse on top of you while you're... you know."

"While I'm eating your sweet, tight, little pussy," he said with a lascivious grin.

She gawked at his blunt words.

"You are a pig!" Alexandra insulted as she slapped his bicep hard.

"I can live with that."

Quickly, he helped her to the makeshift bed he had made on the floor. Arranging her on her back with her long, graceful legs slightly bent at the knees and feet flat for stability, placing the towel beneath her, just in case.

"Believe me, you love it when I do this." Before she could reply, he was using his thumbs to spread her lower lips, the evidence of her arousal glistening on her puffy folds. "You're so pink, like cotton candy, but sweeter."

Immediately, her body suddenly stiffened.

"What's the matter?" he frowned.

"Nobody's ever seen me naked before, except my gynecologist," she explained, her expression glum. "I know I'm not a *Victoria Secret* supermodel. My tummy is a little soft, and I could lose about ten pounds. I think it's from those muffins I like so much, and I know I should probably exercise… and my breasts… well, just look at them—"

Interrupting her rant he teased, "You're rambling."

"I know, but just look at them." She stuck her chest out further. The movement made his member even harder, and he realized she didn't know the power she held over him. Over his head. Over his dick. But most importantly, over his heart.

"I love you," he reminded. "I fantasize about your breasts, and right now I can't take my eyes off of them. I think every inch of you is amazing. I just want to eat you up."

She tried to comment, but he interrupted once more.

"Just. Like. This." He punctuated each word with a flick of his tongue to the swollen bud at the apex of her thighs.

"Roman," she hissed, the tiny licks sending her body into overdrive.

He held her thighs with a firm grip knowing that the moment his mouth made contact again she would try to slam them together.

"Don't fight it, *relax*," he implored.

Her body softened a little.

"There you go. Look at me." The words didn't quite register until his mouth came down once again, latching onto her lower lips.

"*Holy shit!*" she whimpered, legs beginning to shake, and she was thankful she was lying down.

Adjusting his shoulders, he used them as a wedge between her widely spread legs as he began a slow exploration of her sex. Licking and sucking and nipping at her folds, then spearing the talented muscle and fucking her with gusto. Alexandra gifted him with another shuddering whimper.

"Delicious," he moaned against her throbbing sex. His chin, lips, and cheeks glistening in the candlelit room. He resumed his task, but this time he used a thick finger to slowly enter her channel, her cream allowing him to slide all the way in to the third knuckle.

"*Shit!*" she exclaimed at the unfamiliar invasion.

"Relax, my love." He continued stroking her there, in and out, in and out, with a slow, steady rhythm that he knew was driving her closer and closer to the edge of reason. When her body was no longer tense, he added a second finger, eagerly stroking her sex trying to find the right spot that would send her into a sexual orbit.

"That... feels... so... *Ah!*" Her legs tried to slam shut, almost locking him to her like a steel vise.

"Are you okay?" Roman questioned.

She nodded.

"You're not holding your breath, are you?" he asked.

This time she shook her head, making him feel less worried. Finally, he added a third finger, the addition causing her to tense up again.

"Breathe through it, Sunshine."

"It feels strange," she moaned, lifting her butt off the sheet. "But good. Don't stop. It'll take me a moment to get use to the sensation."

Resuming his task, he worked his thick digits into her core. Slowly at first, then picked up speed until Alexandra was writhing and squirming and moaning dirty words like a veteran sailor. When he felt her inner muscles begin to squeeze and tense, he bent, adding hummingbird-quick flicks to the bud peeking out from under its hood.

"Roman," she keened, grabbing a handful of his hair in one hand.

"Stop holding back and just enjoy it, my love," he begged.

"I think... I'm... *coming!*" she yelled, fingers clawing at the silk sheet with the other hand.

With practiced perfection, he sucked her clit between his lips using his mouth to create a steady suction. That was all she needed to push her into oblivion. As the orgasm barreled into her like a freight train, he pushed in as far as he could, found her maidenhead, and with a scissoring-motion pushed through the barrier.

"What the—" her complaint halted as she noticed the slight pain at being breached. The tensing of muscles inside her channel almost broke his fingers. Ripples of her passion shimmied from her sex to her abdomen then outward until every limb shivered from the bliss it created.

"Alexandra are you sure you're alright?" he asked again.

His chest tightened at the pain she must be feeling. There was no sound.

"Alexandra, damn it! Answer me. How are you?"

"Wow!" she exclaimed in a loud, throaty whisper. "Now, I know what all of the fuss is about."

A large grin spread across her illuminated face like a light had been turned on beneath her skin.

"You can do that to me anytime."

Roman went to his knees, his face tense with need. The need to have her. Every soft, pliable inch of her.

"That was just the beginning," he informed as he fitted himself between the vee of her thighs. "We haven't even started the good stuff yet."

His raspy tone creating another set of ripples, but this time they were heading down to her sex.

"I'm still nervous," she admitted without shame, her lustful state quickly dissipating.

"To tell the truth, I'm nervous too." His lips set in a thin, hard line.

"Why are you nervous?" Her hands guided of their own accord to his abdomen, playing with the lean muscles they found there.

"If I'm terrible, you'll always remember it because I was your first," he explained.

He gently pushed her legs further apart, exposing her completely to his gaze. The sight of her so vulnerable made his heart ache and his body tense.

"This is the only part of this whole fucking *déjà vu* thing that I ever want to experience again."

She giggled, the sound tickling his ears. Alexandra looked like a goddess against the black shiny satin sheet. Her onyx locks spread around her head like an enticing veil, eyes twinkling with desire. With need.

He missed the luxuriousness of his king-sized bed, but the only thing that truly mattered was being here with her.

Looking around he proclaimed, "It's not the Waldorf—"

"It's better," she soothed. "Stop worrying about every little thing, Roman, and make love to me."

Eagerly, he touched her, adjusting her legs until they were spread as wide as they could with her legs bent at the knees.

"As I was saying, before my woman so rudely interrupted."

She opened her mouth to argue, but he continued.

"Yes, I said *my woman*. You are, ya know."

Alexandra's eyes narrowed, but her smile said everything she felt.

"No other man will ever touch you like this. I intend to be the only one, *ever*."

"That's very presumptuous of you," her words came without heat.

Her best friend pouted.

"What makes you think I want you, long term that is?" she asked with a chuckle. "You can be a real pain in the ass."

"Shh," he tweaked the tip of her nose. "I'm still explaining."

She laughed at his playfulness. A playful Roman was a heart-stopping, sexy Roman and she loved sexy Roman. *A lot!*

"Sorry, go ahead with your explanation," she urged, pursing her lips, pretending to lock them and throw away the invisible key.

He continued.

"If I'm really good," he grinned and arched one brow. "Then I'll forever be remembered as the only man who rocked your world so thoroughly that you won't be able to look at another man without comparing him to me."

The thought of her being his forever made him smile.

Alexandra giggled, the sound making his cock flex like it was being controlled by some horny puppet master.

"I'll have to rename you. Let's see, you'll be—"

"Roman, Italian god of sex, and all things naughty," he finished with an omniscient smirk.

"Exactly," she agreed.

"Damn straight." He chuckled. "I can't wait any longer."

She nodded, body tensing again.

"Stop holding your breath and just relax, Sunshine," he smirked. "It's no fun if you're unconscious."

She glared at him.

"That's easy for you to say, you're not the one getting ready to be impaled by a blunt projectile. If I had known you had *that*, in your pants I wouldn't have agreed so easily."

She took a deep, steadying breath, then released it in a slow, but steady stream.

"Okay," she announced, squeezing her eyes shut like she was bracing for a shot or something equally unpleasant. "Just do it."

"I keep telling you, this isn't a shoe commercial." He smoothed back the black tresses that were clinging to her flushed cheeks. "I want it to be incredible for you. Do you trust me?"

She nodded without hesitation causing his chest to do that strange tightening thing it had been doing all day long whenever they were in the same room.

"Kiss me," she ordered with a slight smile. "Now, before I change my mind."

He didn't have to be told twice. Bending slightly, he took her lips again, placing soft kisses at the sides of her mouth.

"Mmm, your lips are so soft, Alexandra."

"Stop talking and take me."

She wiggled her naked form against him, her soft breasts smashing against his much harder chest. The warmth from the candles and from the hot woman beneath him made him perspire, but he didn't care.

Releasing her lips he made his way down her body, bypassing all of the other tasty parts of her form until he ended at the entrance of where he was dying to be. Slowly, his fingers parted her folds and without hesitation he sunk one long, thick, finger into her hot, wet depths.

"You're ready, and you're so hot and tight," he hissed, unable to think clearly as her flesh hugged his digit.

"Good grief, Roman," she moaned. Her entire body going rigid as anticipation registered in her lust-hazed brain. Slowly, Roman began to ease it out, not quite removing it completely, then leisurely pushed it back inside of her entrance all the way to the second knuckle.

"Why are you doing this again?"

"I need you to be ready for me because I don't know how much self-control I'm gonna have once I'm inside your tight little pussy."

"Makes sense," she stiffened.

# Four Past Midnight

"Breathe, Sunshine... breathe." he ordered, the scent of hot, aroused woman filling his nostrils and pushing him closer to the animal need to claim her hard.

After a few seconds, her body relaxed, and her legs actually widened for him as her hips began a slow circular motion against his hand.

"Don't stop," she commanded on a low, husky growl.

Quickly, he adjusted himself, leaned forward and gave one of her tightened nipples several long, sinewy, swipes with his tongue. The flavor of Alexandra hiking up his arousal another notch as his cock grew agonizingly harder.

*Fuck!* He was in so much pain he thought he'd die from it.

Almost withdrawing his finger completely, she pushed up onto her elbows and gave him a sullen pout making him chuckle. Without warning, he added a second finger into her channel, amazed at the tight fit. He knew he'd be able to fit all of himself inside the extremely tight confines of her body.

*Fuck yeah! It would be a snug fit, to say the least.*

If he died from the pleasure of being inside her then so be it.

Finally, he added a third finger, sliding in and out of her a little easier due to the sweet cream weeping from her core.

"Sunshine, you're drenched. I'm soaked with your cream. Are you ready for me?" he asked, hoping the answer was a resounding *'yes'*.

The nod of her head and the heated gaze she graced him with was the only answer he needed.

Without further ado, he knelt between her spread legs, took his unyielding length in his hand, noticing crimson streaks, the evidence of her virginity on his fingers. Reaching down deep into his soul, he prayed for the ability to not take her like a primal beast.

Taking a steadying breath, he lined his cockhead to her sopping sex, holding it firmly at the base, and then swiping it through her folds coating it with her cream which was easy since she was so turned on.

Gradually, he began to push inside, stopping when he was only a couple of inches in. Both of their eyes widened as the tip of his cock entered her virgin space. Before her panic could take voice, he pushed in another inch. Her body turned to marble as her knees locked his hips in place. Eyes widened to the size of saucers as she held her breath.

He had to ease her discomfort.

"I've never been this out of control except with you. Did you know that?"

She shook her head.

"Well, it's true."

He pulled his hips back allowing it to slide out about an inch and then pushed back inside.

"I'm not rational when it comes to you. You know those guys you interviewed today?"

She nodded yes.

"I told you to do phone interviews because I didn't want them lusting after you. The thought of them looking at you made me jealous. Are you surprised that I'm territorial when it comes to you?"

"Yes," she spoke on a whisper, her nails digging into the tops of his shoulders.

"I want us to be together," he poured out his intentions. "Not just as friends."

"I might agree to that," she said, eyes glistening in the surrounding candlelight.

"Might?" His heart clenched.

She smiled.

"It depends on how good you are in bed," she told, waggling her brows playfully.

"Let me give you a sample of what you can expect," he grinned roguishly, kissing the tip of her nose.

"Roman—" her sentence ended abruptly as he pushed past her tightly gripping inner muscles.

"You can take me," he proclaimed softly, the tight fit even tighter than he remembered.

"Roman," Alexandra moaned and tried to close her legs, her motion stopping him from entering any further. He bent, claiming her lips and demanding entrance. A second later, she opened for him, and he didn't miss a beat.

Instantly, he found her tongue, lavishing it with wet lashes and long sucks on the tip he hoped would drive her into a sexual frenzy. Of course, he was right. Thank goodness! Her legs relaxed once again, and he pushed in a little further until almost half of his hard-as-nails member was seated.

"Damn it!" Her lower body lifted from the comforter in a spasm, and she chastised against his lips. "You're too big!"

He gritted his teeth before saying, "Should I stop?"

*Please don't say 'yes.'*

When she didn't say anything else he tried to push in another inch, and both of their eyes widened again. Reaching between their bodies, he located the tiny bud at the apex of her thighs. Coating his finger in her cream, he started to draw invisible circles on her clit with the tip of his middle finger. He breathed a sigh of relief when another trickle of her arousal coated his shaft. Instinctively, he pulled out again, just an inch or so and then pushed back in another couple of inches, continuing the circular motion with his finger.

"That feels so wicked," she moaned, arching her back off of the sheet. Her more than ample breasts tempting him to have a taste, so he did.

Abandoning her full, pouty lips he bent lower, surrounding her beaded cotton-candy-pink nipple with his mouth. Using his tongue, he teased and licked the delicious nub. When she arched more, he closed his lips around it and began a steady sucking motion causing it to harden even further.

"I'm never gonna get enough of you, Miss Martin," he moaned against her overheated flesh, the vibration making her squirm with need.

Releasing the peak he went for its twin, licking and sucking until she began to meet him stroke for agonizing stroke. He paused briefly.

"It's gonna take a lifetime for me to get you out of my system. I hope you don't have any plans for the next fifty years or so."

Her huge grin dazzled him.

Quickening his pace, he fought his way inside her heat and sighed as he was finally... *finally*... fully seated... balls deep. The sudden realization hit him hard. He was buried to the hilt inside of his woman, his little piece of sunshine. Smiling, he began to move.

*He was in fucking paradise.*

"Don't stop," she pleaded, her strained voice bringing him back to reality.

He began to really move then, withdrawing and advancing, finding that wonderful pace that made her moan and him curse. Being inside the tight space was both pleasure and pain, agony and ecstasy. Her body gripped him like a tight vise giving him no quarter. And her moans... her moans were the most erotic sound he'd ever heard. Soft sighs of passion and deep growls of lust. She was made for him.

"Look at me, Sunshine," he commanded, wanting, no needing to see her when she came. Needing her to know that he was the one to take her to the edge of reason. "I want you to remember this moment, always. When we're old and gray and I need male enhancement drugs to do this, I want you to remember the first time we made love."

She smiled as she pulled his mouth back to hers. Her insistent tongue slipped past his defenses as she sucked the tip of his tongue into her mouth, applying a steady suction that reminded of what she had done to his cock earlier. That was all it took.

"Alexandra, I can't holdback anymore."

The tightening of his balls warned of his eminent release.

"I need you to come," he announced as his hips began a wild pounding into her clenching depths.

"*Roman!*" she yelled, body tensing, her back leaving the floor almost bucking him off. At the same instant, hot jets of molten seed shot into her hungrily clenching core, the sensation of tiny fingers forcing all of his manhood into her. He collapsed on top of her, shifting his body to the side so he could press against her still heaving bosom without crushing her.

"You are amazing every time. Amazing." Words finally came to him. Not the eloquent ones he hoped for, but the only ones he could currently form.

"I never... *ever*... thought it would be so—" Her breathing returned to normal, as they held each other.

"Life changing?" he finished her thought.

"Uh-huh," she replied rolling to her side, the feeling of warmth engulfing him. "You wore me out, sex-fiend."

Chuckling at her softly spoken words he adjusted his body, so her head was cradled in the crook of his arm, those delicious breasts smashed against his side.

"I wore *you* out?" he teased, "I had to do all of the work."

"I worked." She slapped him lightly on the chest.

"Moaning and making all of those erotic sounds doesn't count," Roman countered with a huge grin.

"Ungrateful," she laughed, enjoying their easy banter. "I'm thinking a nap sounds good."

# Four Past Midnight

*"Mmm,"* he agreed closing his eyes, his arm wrapped around her shoulder. "A nap sounds really good."

It was the last thing he said before falling into a peaceful slumber.

# XIII

The rest of the day was perfect. They woke around seven in the evening and made love in the shower. Got dressed, saw a movie and went to the Sweetshop Café for a late dinner. Roman couldn't have imagined a better way to spend time with the woman he loved.

"You're addicted to those things," he taunted, eyeing Alexandra's chocolate chip muffin she had bought for later.

"Stop complaining," she admonished without heat. "You'll be extremely happy I bought it when we're watching Forever Knight and you want something to nibble on."

"Sunshine," he growled, bending low and placing a wicked kiss to her barely parted lips.

She tasted of strawberries, chocolate, and her unique flavor. It was intoxicating and he couldn't wait to get back to his place, which was closer.

"I'll have you to nibble on."

Smacking his arm playfully as she cooed, "I can't wait."

Her hand disappeared behind her back, and he jumped at the unexpected pinch she gave his bottom.

"I think I've created a monster." He laughed.

# Four Past Midnight

"You have indeed." Her eyes twinkled with desire.

"Let's get to my apartment fast," he begged, his mind wandering to sensual images.

"All right," she said with a breathy sigh.

"What time is it?" Roman questioned, realizing he had forgotten his wristwatch. "I need to take Bruno out first before I have my way with you again."

She blushed before glancing down at her watch.

"It's four past midnight."

Her head cocked to the side when his eyes grew large, an unknown emotion on his handsome face.

"Maybe we should…"

The crosswalk signal changed to green and without checking she made a motion to step off of the sidewalk into the road.

"Alexandra!" he yelled, his heart throbbing in his ears. *"Stop!"*

Instinctively, Roman's arm darted out, his body amped-up on adrenaline, grabbed her around the waist and pulled her back just in time to save her from the speeding car running through the red light as they attempted to cross the street.

"What the—" she gasped as the car's tires sprayed them with dirty water.

"Hey, you idiot! We're walking here!" Roman bellowed at the driver, flicking him off at the same time.

His usually dormant New York accent accosting her ears since they were huddled so close together under the extra-large umbrella. A second later a police siren blared, and, in the distance, they could see the driver being pulled over, removed from the car, handcuffed, and deposited into the police car.

A thankful smile appeared on Roman's face.

"Remind me why I moved to this city," she said, trying to ignore her soaking wet trouser legs. Thank goodness her raincoat covered to her knees. Roman, on the other hand, was drenched from head to toe.

"Because you wanted to be a world-class journalist with the four-one-one on all of the biggest and best news stories," he reminded with a frown trying not to shiver. "And as luck would have it, your best friend is the editor of The Citywide Chronicle and didn't think twice about hiring you. Even though, you technically have no real experience as a reporter."

She tapped her bottom lip with her index finger. The motion made his cock grow to a semi-hard position.

"I suppose all of that is correct," she conceded. "I knew it would be worth keeping you around."

"You're such a nerd," he teased. "But you're my nerd, and I love you."

"I love you too, Roman. Now, take me home and make love to me." She waggled her perfectly shaped eyebrows making him laugh.

"I really have created a monster. Let's go, sex-fiend."

## Four Past Midnight

His entire body tingled as they pressed together beneath the umbrella.

Them. Together. It was kismet.

And it was wonderful.

# EPILOGUE

*Beep! Beep! Beep!*

Roman woke with a start, heart beating hard against his sweat-covered chest. Looking around, he glared at the damn alarm clock. It was four past midnight.

*Why the hell was his alarm clock going off now?*

Quickly, he stood and looked at the ground for his pants.

*Wait! Where were his pants?*

The muffled sound of the toilet flushing startled him. He realized then that light was coming from beneath the bathroom door. Cautiously, he ran to the walk-in closet, fumbled around in the dark space looking for—

*Ah ha!*

His *Louisville Slugger* was hidden behind his dress shoes. With frayed nerves, he gripped the handle and pulled it out.

Silently, he stalked to the slightly ajar bathroom door, and rested his ear on the cool wooden surface, before giving the barrier a gentle, but firm nudge. The soft squeak startled the intruder making the person jump.

"Roman!" Alexandra shouted, her hands grasping her belly.

# Four Past Midnight

Instantly, his eyes focused again on her and her large, rounded belly.

"You scared the stuffing out of me!" she chastised loudly. "Stop doing that!"

Overjoyed to see her, he exhaled, and a sense of relief washed over him at the sight of her alive and carrying their child.

"What are you doing in there?"

Alexandra looked delicious in her pastel blue maternity sleepshirt.

"What do you think I'm doing in here?" she asked sarcastically with a wide, toothy grin.

His frown made her laugh.

"I had to use the bathroom." Automatically, her slender hand caressed her tummy. "Mister Giordano, *Junior* is sitting on my bladder, and he won't move."

Tired and uncomfortable, she turned off the light and kissed her husband on his overheated cheek.

"He's stubborn like his daddy." She giggled, the sound going straight to his groin.

Instantly, he was at half-mast.

Looking down at the impressive bulge tenting his boxer briefs, she sighed.

"Not now, sex-fiend. I'm exhausted. Maybe in the morning."

While she waited for him to join her, she snuggled under the covers, patting the empty space beside her for him to hurry.

"Roman, why are you carrying that bat?"

In a haze as well, he glanced down at the bat in his hand, and began to laugh.

"The alarm startled me, and I thought I was stuck in that freaking time-loop nonsense again, but then I saw the light on, and I didn't remember I have a wife now and—"

She smiled and his ramble instantly ceased.

"Oh," she said with a grin, patting the mattress again. "Come back to bed."

Happily, he dropped the bat to the floor before joining his gorgeous wife below the covers, pulling her more firmly against his side, and waited as her arms wrapped around his waist.

*"Mmm,"* he hummed against the top of her hair.

His fingers playing with the silky strands as she cuddled with him.

"Did you have that nightmare again?" she asked, her fingers running up and down his breastbone, a very distracting sensation.

"No," he said truthfully. "I forgot *when* I was."

Her eyes narrowed with confusion.

"Never mind," he insisted, kissing the top of her head. "I just had a flashback."

He smiled, his eyes closing once again.

"I'm sorry the alarm clock woke you. Isn't that my three dollar one?"

# Four Past Midnight

He nodded yes.

"I swear that thing has a mind of its own," his wife replied, placing her hand over his heart, enjoying the way it pounded against her palm. "Try to go back to sleep."

"I love it when you boss me around," he stated mischievously, eyes still closed, his breathing becoming shallower. "Have I told you lately how much I love you, Missus Giordano?"

"Yes." She giggled, closing her eyes as well. "Every single day."

**The End!**

# ABOUT THE AUTHOR

L. D. K. Johnson is an American author hailing from the East Coast of the U.S., where she enjoys spending time with family and friends when she is not sitting in front of her laptop writing the next book that comes to mind. Her favorite things in life are chocolate, creamer (not necessarily coffee), and anything D.I.Y. related.

L. D. K. Johnson first made her mark on the writing scene with her beloved contemporary erotic romance books, The Kapahu Series, set on the beautiful Hawaiian island of Oahu. Ms. Johnson followed with Counting Stars, Four Past Midnight, and the first installment of her adult Fantasy series, Lup Teren (Wolf Land Series).

After a several year hiatus from writing, L. D. K. is ready to jump back into the fray; wowing fans with sexy new stories, but not without a reintroduction of her prior books in a new home.

# L. D. K. JOHNSON TITLES

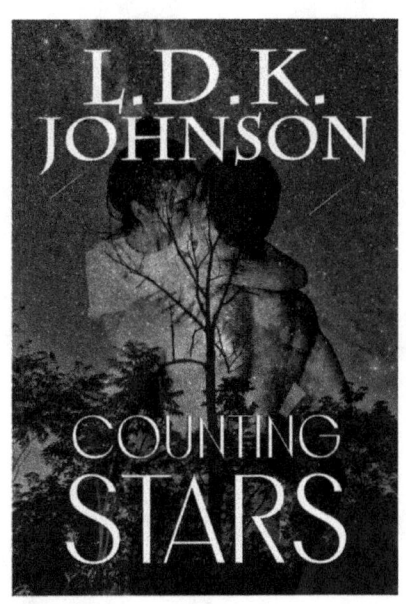

### AVAILABLE EVERYWHERE!